Night Snip

Night Ship

A Voyage of Discovery

Mattie McClane
Myrtle Hedge Press

Night Ship, A Voyage of Discovery

Copyright © 2017, 2003 by Myrtle Hedge Press

ISBN 978-0-9722466-5-1

Library of Congress Control Number 2017911607

Myrtle Hedge Press
Kernersville NC

Contents

Preface

I shared the manuscript of this novel with Alison Lurie at her seaside residence in Wrightsville Beach, North Carolina in the spring of 1999. Ms. Lurie gave me directions to her rented home, but the beach houses looked the same. I became lost and was late for our meeting.

When I explained my predicament to the novelist, she said, "You're lost because you don't have your navigator with you." I laughed. Still, her statement suggested that I was Galveo, the captain of *Night Ship*. I suppose that being an author is very much like being a captain of an exploration ship: one directs the plot through numerous ideas; occasionally one experiences verbal doldrums and swift changes in currents. But am I Galveo?

I am Galveo, as the French novelist Gustave Flaubert was Madame Bovary. As the author of *Night Ship, A Voyage of Discovery,* I share some affinity with all my created characters. I understand Galveo's tendency for romance, for the dreamy way she looks at her circumstances. I share her love of poetry. I sympathize with Sella's no-nonsense, up-from-the-bootstraps ambition. I imagine Mahajan's sense of being displaced, her painful lot of being "the other" in a strange land. I imagine Nic's battle with felt duty and obligation, her battle with conscience, and other people's demands on her time. I admire Melody's kindness and her wisdom. I feel sorry for Trinket's loneliness, and the way that objects become the center of her emotional life.

Night Ship, A Voyage of Discovery, is a short novel with a two-part structure. Six women, unknown to each other by day, join each other in a common dream or mythos aboard a fifteenth century sailing ship. Each character narrates a twenty-first century story and also a fantasy story on the boat. The sailing ship is meant to represent the Lacanian concept of desire for the mother and is further influenced by Julia Kristeva's theory of the semiotic. The fantasy section constitutes the maternal division of language. The collective dream is fluid and rhythmic; the mythos is the realm of color and aspects of visual language. It is the realm of both spirituality and sexuality. It is the place of lesbian desire.

There are six main characters. Their life situations are as follows: Anna is a writer. Sella is a software designer. Mahajan is a dishwasher in a restaurant. Nic is a newspaper editor. Melody is an aspiring singer. Trinket owns a junk shop.

In the fantasy section, Anna Galveo is the captain of Night Ship. Sella is the brilliant and short-tempered navigator. Mahajan is the storytelling helmswoman. Nic is the proud and practical mechanic. Melody is the kind scribe. Trinket is the playful half-wit with a penchant for things.

Anna's mother gives her an antique globe on Christmas Eve. Unable to obtain her father's love, Anna dreams of being the captain of Night Ship. The 1957 globe takes on heightened meaning in the fantasy section: it could be a hoax or the knowledge of the known world.

The future is in the past. At last, the two-part structure collapses, and "the sea" and "home" are joined in the characters' minds. The only power left on the boat is the power of redeeming love.

M.M.
Greensboro, NC
July 15, 2002

Galveo

I bought my father life jackets for Christmas. The thought of the gift made me shudder. They would stack up queerly upon the usual gifts from the others. My father often received gold-toed socks and white dress shirts striped with thin blue. One by one, the gifts from his other children would accumulate, and then there would be life jackets.

Snowflakes crowded into the headlights of a Dodge Caravan. A semi-trailer creeped ahead of it. Tire tracks sliced the snow into segments. The shiny paths occasionally ran off the road suggesting the movement of a butter square on a heated skillet, turning, slipping, turning again.

Wayward cars were in the ditches and on the median.

"Will Frank be at your parents' Christmas Eve party?"

My brother Frank wouldn't be home. Frank had moved to Jakarta as part of his promotion. He was now vice president of the international group for a major communications corporation. He had a driver, a cook, a gardener.

"How about Joey?" Rich said.

"Joey will be there," I told my husband. My mind went through Joey stories. My youngest brother had taken a job with a firm in rural Illinois. He now quoted Jesus at the end of legal letters. May you find the blood of Christ. He had attended a Christian men's rally in Washington D.C. in a rented van; its driver took sick, went to rest in the back, and died of a heart attack. The body was flown to Chicago. The faithful group continued on their trek and made the opening ceremonies.

"Dana is in from Ohio," I said. "She's been living in a hotel until she sells her house." Dana directed customer service managers for a department store chain. As a result of her stunning participation in a conference call, she was transferred to a troubled office in Dayton.

"It's the wrong time of year to sell a house with a pool," my husband said. It was the wrong time of the year to buy life jackets. I pushed the thought out of my mind once again.

"I never thought she'd move away," I said. The semi-trailer's red brake lights beamed the snowfall; the heavy flakes designed the view ahead and made it look like a porous fabric, as if gauze had been draped across the windshield. My husband reacted to the truck, and we slowed down.

"Just Joey and Dana?" Rich asked.

"Cindy's home," I said, as if the news weren't news. The year had been full of reports about Cindy. Cindy had failed the bar. Then she passed the bar. My father's office help was up in arms about her starting salary. She had joined my father's law firm and was featured in a town newspaper.

Dana, Me, Frank, Joey and Cindy. That was our birth order. The order of our success was determined on a yearly basis. I was the first child that might have been an attorney. I was the first one to have the career talk with my father at the IHOP over coffee: it was the bottomless conversation in my family. The conversation never ended: it went through wait staffs, seasons, years, and was passed onto the next child like a runner's baton.

Snow covered the fields beside the interstate. There was so much white in the darkness. It could have been a sea. I would have been a sailor on a fine caravel. I dreamed of ships when I thought of my father. I would have been a lawyer to please my father. He was a man who dreamed for his children. His children dreamed that he smiled. But I kept writing stories and imagining galleons clad in gold leaf.

There were deck fighters at swivel guns firing grape-shot. The helmsman was steady and calm. He swung the rudder, changing course. The evasive move was gallant in that there was small need to destroy. The battle was over sovereignty, the idea was to get away. The flagship cut through the blackish blue sea.

"We're going to miss the party," my husband said. "At this rate, we're never going to get there."

"I bought my father life jackets for Christmas," I said as if I were making a confession. "It's winter. Who buys life jackets in December for somebody who lives in Iowa?"

"He has a boat. He'll just put them away until summer. What's the big deal?"

"Maybe it's no big deal. But it's weird." I imagined that the stores would be open on another day, that it was not Christmas Eve, that there would be another chance to buy him a different gift. But time had run out. We were getting closer to Iowa, and we weren't going to miss the party.

"How come you bought them? Did you ever hear your father say that he wanted life jackets?" Rich asked.

In my childhood, my father always wanted his life jackets. He could never find them because Frank and I had them. My brother and I used them to swim in the river. We could float with them and stay in the water for a long while.

We often took our rowboat to the center of the river, jumped over the sides, and swam in the deep water. The water was a relief from the July heat; it was recreation, and a way of escaping our chores. The afternoon sun hit the top of the waves, lighting drops, causing flickerings. Curls of water leaped up and lapped our faces. My father had brought a colleague to the house and had planned to go out on the big boat. The two men stood on the dock, and we heard our father's voice travel across the flat surface of the river. The good life jackets were gone. We heard his angry tone, and it made us come to shore. But how could we give him the life jackets? They were wet, and he'd scream at us for removing them from his boat. At first, we were going to run them back to him. But Frank and I left them on the shore and walked home. It was a joint decision.

Twenty-five years later, in a Walmart, I unwittingly performed an act of restitution, and I now marveled at the staying power of the guilty past. Melted flakes stuck to the window glass, dropping from their weight. Young voices whispered in my mind's ear, and a scene emerged, rolling, then stopping, rolling again. Ice. Water. Summer…

Frank was strapped into an orange pillow and looked like a package ready to be mailed. A bow, shoelace style, was tied underneath his chin. I sat beside him on the center bench of a rowboat. I must have looked the same, all wrapped up, like no sailor, like no captain. I pulled the strings beneath my chin, deciding not to wear the jacket. My arm went behind my head and lifted it; it caught my ears. Frank watched, seemed to think my move was pretty daring, not because I might drown, but because we had been told to wear them.

"I can't wear it," I told my brother. Frank smiled. I raised my oar and we were off, going up river, past summer cabins, to where the cottonwoods were thick. I saw Frank's oar rise and fall with mine. We'd pull together, lean far back, go forward to catch the next wave. Our common effort was important, full of urgency. Explorers claimed places and named them.

Explorers came back with gold. "We need to bring something back," I said.

Frank cocked his head and asked what. He turned to the trees, the mud banks, then said, "Nothing to bring back." But on the shore, between the branches, in the weeds, was an object that appeared to be a box.

"It's a laundry cabinet," I said.

"It won't float," Frank growled.

"Maybe it will," I said. Once in front of Frank's friends, I bet that a container, the kind that electrical workers stood in, would float and spent maybe a half an hour trying to talk somebody into getting in it. Nobody would; I did and it sunk. Poor Frank didn't understand my wish to make boats. But Frank didn't know many stories, only the ones that I told him. My brother knew rules, instructions, how to hang a rake. Still I thought I might convince him that stories were rules, that in stories like a law, things always happened the same way.

Frank liked my stories about explorers. I told him the story, and he would pretend it with me.

"It looks like a canoe," I said. Frank's eyes were interested. We rowed away from the tree, now pulling the aluminum cabinet at an angle; its ends were square, and if we kept rowing, water would come over its top. "We'll have to float it back," The cabinet lagged behind. Its seams were rusty and broken, and it was heavy from the leaks. I picked up my life jacket, fussing with the straps, stringing the thing around my neck. Frank gave me a funny look, seemed to laugh at me, and he knew we were getting close to home. "Don't laugh," I told him, thinking that we both knew the rules about being on the river…

All my father's rules. A fat speckle fell like a star. How I bawled at Frank's wedding. The bridesmaids walked in measured steps up to the altar, and their dyed shoes seemed to imprint the carpet like the cut-out footsteps of a dance lesson. One gown was pastel green, the next was lavender. A single flower adorned their hats. The women were like tall adolescents made up by their mothers for Easter. They were a hideous group: At least they looked hideous on the day that Frank was married. It was an outrage to cry for a betrothed brother. My relatives told me this with every quick glance.

But he was my map-maker. Frank was Bartholomew when I was Christopher Columbus. I set sail on one of Genoa's merchant ships. He stayed behind to draw maps on a flat and heavy table. I consulted him first about my plan to go to China. Tears stained my dress. I looked at my mother's rose corsage.

An interstate sign shot by. Blue and yellow lights flashed in the distance, creating a mysterious object; a tow truck and a snowplow seemingly merged into the same space, were separated only by our increasing proximity.

"If you don't want to give your father life jackets, didn't you bring Frank's present?" My husband hinted at a solution to my dilemma.

"Give my father what I bought for Frank?"

"Yeah," Rich said.

"No," I said. "Who knows? My father may have been waiting for this gift for years."

Dana passed out the presents. I followed the life jackets from their spot under the tree to my father. I saw the frozen river and its new surface of snow through the large picture window.

I watched my father remove the wrapping. One of Cindy's kids shrieked with excitement. I only looked away for a moment, and I missed it. The life jackets were opened. They were set beside my father's chair. Rich came to sit beside me. My father waited for my husband to become situated, then he said to Rich, "Thank you for the life jackets." Dana stopped in front of me, letting down a present. The bright and colorful box blocked my view of my father.

Mother moved closer to me. "Open it," she said with her eyes glistening. I stood and pulled at the sealed cardboard. I tugged at a faded curtain. The yellow cloth served as packing for an antique globe; its oceans, once blue, were dark green from age. The globe rested on a heavy solid circle of brass.

"I thought it would look nice in your study," my mother said.

"Thank you," I told her. I looked over to my father who held up a robe. His smile was huge and was directed at Dana. He set one of Cindy's children on his lap. His head bent down near the child's lips as if he were listening. I spun the globe. Seven continents and five oceans. The robe covered the life jackets. Nothing could be given or taken back now; the time had passed, and the distance between Father and me was too great. I searched the globe's print for its date: 1957.

That night in my sleep, I was Anna Galveo. I was a captain sworn to King John I in 1488 and was commissioned to find new lands for the glorious Crown. The rain swatted my back, nearly pushed me through my cabin's door. The Crown navigator came in behind me. There was a flurry of motion as we shook off the weather from our coats. The storm was furious; the waves raged at and tossed the Night Ship. Great sprays hurled their way onto the deck where we spent most of the night. "The wind is dying," I said. "It's going to pass." I removed two linen shirts from the drawer beneath my bunk. I changed from my wet garments and hoped for a few hours of rest before the sun came up.

Sella took off her shoes, stepping down on the back of her boot with the heel of the other.

My limbs were as tired as rags. I uncorked a skin of madeira and poured the liquid into metal cups. The rock of the ship moved the wine so that its surface quivered. Sella came down and sat beside me; we drank. We drank silently: exhaustion had taken our words. The smell of drenched wool and leather filled the small space. I brushed the drying strands of hair from Sella's face. My body was heavy like an already sunken stone, held in place at every point by an invisible force. My thoughts were sinking as well.

"Galveo, are you ever afraid?" Sella said.

"Of the ocean?" I thought about the power of the gales, the sprays' force against my weight. Sella moved closer to me. I put the palm of my hand on her cheek, touching both the bottom of her jaw and her temple. "When my footing slips in the wash, I am afraid. We're fortunate when we are enough. Are you frightened, Sella?"

"Not of the storm," she whispered to me. Her eyelids drooped and then lifted. "Do hold me," she said. I put my arms around her loosely and wondered about the duration of her vulnerability: how long would it last? Her fatigue was a part of it, accounting for her tenderness. I resolved to let the moment be. I felt her breath on my shirt and knew that I was warming a tired wildcat.

I was awakened by intent knocks. "Galveo," a voice said from behind the door. Light burst through the opening, blinding me for a moment.

"The sun is up, and you must tell us about our way," Nic said.

Thank you Nic. Sella's eyes were set in a stare as if they were fixed jewels. Quickly she rose and moved at a fantastic speed.

"Galveo, I'll set the rudder," she said and was off. Sella was discussing the ship's course with Mahajan. A map scroll was underneath one of her arms, and she pointed at the sun with the other. Then her gesture fell and swept widely across the horizon line. The helmswoman nodded as if she understood what Sella had directed. I walked to Mahajan.

The Indian woman shook her head. "Sella asked me to tell her if you ordered a changed course," Mahajan said.

"She's a brilliant navigator. But I think the rudder should shift a few degrees." The Indian woman stepped aside, and I adjusted the course. Mahajan frowned at being in the middle of our disagreements. "I'll talk to Sella," I said. I smiled. Mahajan mumbled at my cheerfulness.

Melody was at the bow, playing her violin. I stood for a minute and listened to a soft song. She stopped playing. "Galveo," she said. "Are you ready to write an entry in the journal?"

"I don't know the ship's damage. I need to talk to Trinket and Nic. Bring your pen to my cabin later in the day. The damage is my first worry," I said.

Nic came up beside me, glaring at Melody's instrument. "Will you see the rigging on the mainsail? It ripped away last night, but I fixed it," the mechanic said. I nodded and followed Nic to the middle of the ship.

Trinket was dancing in circles like a child who delighted in lone play. Her yellow hair stuck out in shoots, as if it were a patch of seedlings. Bangles and spangles were on her arms; jewels hung down from her earlobes. I arched my neck to see Nic's repairs.

"Do you want to climb the ropes?" Nic asked. The sails were taut and full of wind. "

"No Nic, I trust your work." I turned to Trinket. "What about the supply area down below?"

"Below is a mess," Trinket said. She brought her arms down from a twirl, and her lips formed a pout. "The beads rolled out on the floor. I need help, Galveo. I can't clean them up by myself."

"Trinket," I said. "Please sweep the beads. You wouldn't want to lose them or have the goats eat them." I raised an eyebrow, hoping to suggest a picture of horror, her beloved beads reduced to animal fodder.

"The goats!" she said and scurried away.

I returned to my cabin and locked the door. The 1957 globe. I jangled through my keys, then unlocked the door. I separated keepsakes until I came to a wooden box, and pulled the crate into the open. I found my hammer and pried the nails from its lid. There were gouges around the container's rim from the other times that I had opened it. I sat the globe on the table, then ran my hands over its smooth top. Seven continents and five oceans. The globe marked cities and states unknown to me. Written on its surface might be the accrued knowledge of generations. If the information could be verified, a small state might become a vast empire. The thought made me somewhat giddy.

I would set the ship on course to find one of its charted islands. Only then would I know what was in front of me. There was a knock. I heard Melody's voice; she wanted to write the details of the storm in the ship's record. It was Melody who presented me with the mysterious globe. One time ashore, she was looking for shells after the tide. She hurt her foot on the exposed corner of the crate. Mahajan and Nic took shovels and unburied the box. The ship's crew thought nothing of it.

"Are you alone?" I said.

"Yes," Melody told me. I opened the door slightly, then more fully, and she entered. I wrapped the globe in linen and returned it to its crate, and nailed its lid. The scribe watched me situate the box in my cabinet. She was sworn to silence about the globe's possibilities.

She thumbed through poetry and was waiting for me. "What will you do with it?"

"I'll find out if it's true," I said.

"Be careful Anna Galveo. The idea takes much of you. Let it only have a little." Melody stopped speaking, but I could tell that she wanted to say more. I looked into her eyes for a longer time than on most occasions and tried to understand her warning. I felt as if my hand was inches away from a summit stone, but my footing rested on a broken and rocky shelf. My emotions alternated between excitement and dread. Kings and queens would vie for the globe, set their fleets at war for it. Or it might be nothing. The memory of Jimmy Jack came to me. Jimmy Jack was a renegade captain who scorned the word "empire" and spoke of the humanity of native peoples. I remembered his eloquent speech at the Crown academy, how the King's guards arrested him and then put him in fetters. But Jimmy's good nature and love of sport had earned him a faithful crew. At Jimmy's trial, his crew overpowered the court's officers and returned the rebel captain to his ship.

At the Crown captains' academy, Jimmy's ideas about discovery were called foolish: Jimmy had suggested that no land could be discovered because it was already claimed by its inhabitants. The Crown reminded us of Jimmy's love of games, his particular love of small bouncing balls: the lecturers said that Captain Jack's mind was untrustworthy, that it was on the level of a child's. A bounty was offered for his demise: the premium was a treasure so large that pirates and sea thugs tracked Jimmy across the ocean. Jack's ship, *Exemption*, was eventually run into the rocks, and the rebel captain was lost. His ideas about all people's freedom were lost, but sea-goers still told of his good nature and love of sport.

He loved to pitch coins. How many nights we tossed coins against the bulwark. How many nights we were together. At first, I ignored his talk against empire and acquisition. It is difficult to imagine one's friend to be an enemy of the Crown. But his talk became more reckless, and we parted ways. What would my dear friend Jimmy think about the 1957 globe?

We began our journal entry. I noted the location of the storm and its vigor. The crew was especially brave, staying on the deck throughout the winds. I estimated how far we had been tossed from our course. Then, after we made our record, Melody taught me about verse and rhymes. She softly read aloud, and I imagined carmine roses. I could almost hear songbirds.

"Galveo!" Sella called me again. "Galveo!" I stood and allowed Sella to enter. She looked at Melody and said, "Go out!" I nodded to Melody, and Sella waited for her to leave the cabin. "You're damned impossible. Everyday I tell Mahajan how to set the rudders, and everyday you change them," Sella said. "Am I not the most skilled navigator on this ship? Do you think I am a fool or are you a fool?"

"I'm looking for the Western passage to the Indies," I said.

"I've mapped the Indies, and I'm telling you that your course is wrong," Sella said. "Where are your calculations, Galveo? Show me your figures!"

She stood in front of the cabinet that hid the globe. "Trust me," I said.

"You're navigating this ship with your heart. Your heart!" Sella said. "I insist that you turn the rudders so that they are in line with my maps. Do you hear me, Galveo?"

"If my course is right, we'll reach a land body in three days," I said. Sella threw up her arms. "If we do not reach land, I'll give you your way," I told the navigator. Sella softened at the thought of control, even if she had to wait a couple of days.

"It's Melody. She's making you silly. Okay then Galveo, you've three days at the most." Her long black braid danced behind her, as she walked out my door and onto deck.

A ship was a pleasant place after a storm; an awakened confidence seemed to lift from the hull inspiring merry thoughts of bountiful islands. The sea had not conquered our vessel but was tamed like a temperamental horse; it bucked, it threw, it whirled until it realized the tenacity of its rider, then a mellowness overcame it, and it could move forward at a gentle stride. I watched the bow cut the ocean and spray long curls to the starboard and the port sides. I extended my telescope full-out and was lost in the vast vision of nothingness, nothing but sea and sky, merging along a thin line, separating by hue.

I capped my scope, tucked it into my belt. I turned my back on the horizon and was now looking at my helmswoman and my mechanic. Nic held a cloth to Mahajan's face. When she took the rag away, I saw a welt on the Indian's cheek. Nic dabbed the cloth in balm and then brought it back to Mahajan's injury. Nic measured the wound with her thumb and index finger. I caught Sella's eye; she was walking towards me, was just past the other two.

Nic picked up a piece of rope, grabbed Sella by the sleeve, pulled back her arm as if she was going to strike the startled navigator. Nic repeated this motion several times to watch Sella flinch. Sella lowered her head, she shrank down low. Nic hoisted the rope at her again and again, although she never really struck Sella. Sella screamed. Nic yelled, "Coward!"

I was lost in Nic's movement, then finally was jolted into action. I ran to Nic, put my hand on her arm and pulled it away; once it slipped loose, but I recovered it and stopped the attack.

"No," I said. "Put down the rope, Nic." I now had the teasing weapon. I let it drop to the deck's floor.

Nic brought Mahajan in front of me. She pointed to her swollen face. "Sella's doing," she said. I looked at Sella. She straightened, stood tall, her chin raised, her furious gaze focused away from her accuser.

"Arrest her, Galveo," she said softly, so that only I might hear.

"What of Mahajan?" I said. I turned Sella to me, and she jerked away. Her arms were folded.

"She disobeyed my order," Sella said. "I told her that she was to tell me of a changed course."

"Mahajan, steady as she goes," I said. "Nic, put away your oil and return to your job." I smiled. I took Sella's arm and began walking her to the bow. I let go of her when she said that she would come willingly. "Shall I have you arrested, Sella?"

Sella rolled her eyes at me. "For what? Whipping a stupid Indian woman?" She laughed. "She'll think twice before she goes over a Crown navigator again," she snorted.

"She did not go over you. I did. You'll be thinking twice before you have any rest on this ship if you keep treating people like you do." I paused. "I don't understand you. You're the most brilliant navigator I've known, and yet you approach others as idiots, simpletons. You could have the respect of the crew for your abilities, but you go on in such a brutish way." I turned her to me. "Nic and Mahajan won't forget the way you go on."

"Have you spotted your island, Galveo?"

"Won't you be kinder to others? I can't defend your violent whims. The crew knows injustice."

"Where is your land body, Anna Galveo? How much respect will the crew have for you after they find that you've taken us off course and on a goose chase. Your goodness, Galveo, will find nothing for the Crown. You're not commissioned to instruct civilized manners!"

"I've two more days," I said.

"Yes," Sella said. "And in two days, you'll finally let me do the work I have trained for. You talk of my brilliance. What whale fat when you play these silly games with me! You treat me like a simpleton and then you ask me to be kind. I am supposed to trust you when what you're doing goes against everything I know. You expect much of me, Galveo." Her gaze was distant now. "Why, I bet that you wish that I were like your Melody and Trinket!" Sella extended her arm and pointed down ship where Trinket was pinning Melody's hair. "Idiots," she said.

"They do their work." I watched Trinket sort and dig through a bucket of hair combs.

"Trinket gives you an exact count of the bells and mirrors, but probably doesn't know how many jars of fresh water are left below. Melody plays that blessed violin, and the strongest wind can't even block out the noise. It annoys me while I am charting the stars."

"You ought to have her play a song for you, go next to her, and really hear what she plays."

Sella smiled. "Really? I suppose next you'll say that Trinket should dress up my hair?" She appeared to be thinking. "If we find an island in two days, Trinket can pin up my hair." She grinned. "But if we don't, Trinket puts your hair into combs. Is that a deal?"

"You may pick the combs, if you promise not to strike any member of my crew again," I said. Sella started walking to Trinket and Melody. She stopped beside Trinket's bucket of combs. She knelt down and looked through her choices, then turned back to me and held up a gaudy piece for me to see. She walked further down the deck, looked back to me, and was gone.

I was up early the next day. The clouds were still on the water and a thick layer of white rose above the mizzenmast. Nic was repairing fishing nets on the deck; the nets were sprawled out from the mainsail to the bow. She walked along the woven fabric, tightening knots and refashioning them where there were holes. In places, she cut the mesh so that its pattern could be made more secure by her nimble and able fingers. Soon Trinket joined her, anticipating the sparkling bellies of the day's catch. Our food supply was low. A steady vertical rain began to fall, presenting a chance to collect fresh water. Trinket hung a tarp so that water trickled down and found a course into a ceramic jar. I walked beside Nic, who then began to tie a knot in the broken web. Nic's fingers turned the net's free strands with amazing quickness.

She looked up to me, her hands busy all the while. "I'd like to boot that woman's hind," Nic said, as she moved forward to the next tear.

"The water seems warm enough for tuna," I said.

Nic was stooped like a duck and waddled forward. "Don't defend her, Galveo. You favor Sella. Sella isn't worth it. It was bad what she did to Mahajan."

"Yes," I said.

"So what you going to do about it?" I was silent. Nic mumbled. "Nothing, that's what," she said. "Nobody on this ship does what she does and gets away with it." Nic looked at me sternly. "That woman is odd."

"She's frustrated," I said.

"Frustrated? Okay. I'm frustrated too. I'm frustrated that these nets are rotting, but that doesn't mean that I take to thrashing."

"Let's throw the nets," I said. I stood. "Trinket, we're going to throw the nets! Help us." Trinket let out a cry, turned in a circle with her arms high in the air. She darted to the bow and picked up the net's lead.

"Wait," said Nic. "The net isn't even fastened to the pulley." Nic turned a rope around a wheel, hooked the net to the ship. "Wait," Nic said again. She tied a final knot. "Okay, let's toss the net." She smiled at the thought. I lifted the center and together we rolled the heavy patterned fabric over the side into the sea.

After a short while, Nic reeled in the nets; squirming with life; turning and stretching as they were set on the deck. Nic opened the net, and Trinket took each creature out into the open and numbered it. She squealed when her count approached fifteen tuna. She skipped forward and back, holding up two fish by their gills. The rain poured down my face, and I wiped it away so that I could better see the delightful scene.

Trinket let the fish down, arranged them in a neat pile. They flipped and flopped as if to get away. "No," Trinket yelled at them. "No! No! No!" Trinket surrounded them with her skittering feet and kept the strays in line. She rubbed their golden and silver skin and seemed to purr with joy at their sight.

"Again!" Trinket picked up the corner of the net. "Throw it again!" Trinket clapped her hands and stomped her feet. Once again, the net was plopped into the sea; the rope went taut.

Trinket called to Melody, who joined us. Trinket took Melody's hands and led her in a dance. The net was brought in. This time it hung loose and still. Trinket stopped dancing and suddenly turned sad. The net was flat, except for a small lump that moved like a beating heart. Nic opened the net, and a bird struggled in place, was unable to walk or fly; it simply quivered and shook. She held the broken tern in her cupped hands; it did no better.

"Land," I said softly.

Melody looked to me. I felt strangely sick and went to my cabin. Melody came after me.

"Galveo!" Melody called after me. I didn't stop, but hurried to my small quarters. She followed me. I sat on my bunk. I put my head into my hands as if it were the sheltered bird in Nic's grasp.

"Your globe is true, Galveo." She sat down beside me, moved my forehead so that she could see my eyes.

"What concerns you?" she said. "Why are you troubled when what you've believed is true?"

"It's a terrible thing to have such knowledge," I said. "It's a responsibility that I don't understand. I don't know what it means for me or for the Crown. I know that the globe is not so simple as the glory of finding new lands. It becomes a power, and I'm scared of it."

"Gifts are well-assigned. If it's a burden, it's a burden you're meant to bear. If it's a joy, then it's yours. Trust yourself, Galveo. Trust that you're the one who needs to keep the knowledge." Melody stopped. "Go celebrate with your crew about an island not so far off! Don't be afraid!"

I stood, smiled at the thought of an island. A celebration was in order. I touched Melody's shoulder. "Thank you," I said.

"Galveo, don't be quick to share your knowledge with your navigator. Do have faith in yourself."

"Yes," I said.

"Still, one island may not be truth. I'll not share the globe with anyone until I'm positive about my find. I'll find the way to other charted lands first. And when the time is right, I'll share what I know."

"That's wise," Melody said.

I nodded. "Let's hope so."

The sails were solid with wind, hard like the vessel itself, moving us ahead toward land, and I ordered that a cask of wine be opened at a first sighting. There was a strong breeze blowing across the deck, cool on my face, whisking my hair, sweeping it to the side. There were moments on a ship when a captain wanted to be alone with her ideas and imaginings. I dreamed of a dark shade of green, the color of the tops of trees. My feet were sometimes on sturdy ground.

The ocean took one away and then pushed one back as if it knew that it was only part of the scheme; it fully recognized the lure of the other half. I turned, and Sella startled me. She had quietly stood beside me, perhaps waiting for my thoughts to clear. "What now, Galveo?" she said.

"What indeed?"

"Well, it seems that you've found your land body," she said softly. She rose to the tips of her boots.

"Still, how do you know that you've found a Western passage to the East Indies? Can I see the calculations that brought you here? Surely that's information you should share with me." I was silent. "You can instruct me," Sella said. I looked straight ahead, wondering what to say, wondering what would satisfy her. "Damn you, Galveo!" she said. "Are you intent on making an ever-lasting fool of me?"

"Look, Sella!" I said. "A rising shade of deeper blue on the horizon!" Sella grabbed my telescope, then brought it down, revealing her full smile. There were several thin lines around her eyes; the light in her eyes flickered; there were dimples in her cheeks. It was a face I had never seen.

"That's it. That's your island!" she said. "It's a land unknown to the Court. It'll bring you honor. Very good," she said. She handed me my scope. She pointed to the Indian woman.

"Shall I tell her or will you?"

"You may tell her," I said.

"Land!" she yelled. "Land!" I turned away from her, looking at the form ahead of us. I felt alone, as if a heavy sense of solitude had driven my voice inward. Yet there was no time to ponder the ramifications of finding the island. The crew anticipated a party of the first sort.

"I, Anna Galveo, the captain of Night Ship, report the discovery of a new island for the Crown of John." Melody penned my words. I stopped. "Perhaps we could do this later. I want to hear a verse." Melody nodded and closed the journal. She brought out a small book, opening it on her lap.

I moved away from my table and sat on the floor, closing my eyes to imagine her words. I saw blue birds diving in the open air, crossing each other's paths. The fields below grew summer grass, green with occasional spots of yellow from the blossoms of daisies. Kindly knights rode through these fields. Then there was a story of a brave king who tracked a dragon, a huge lizard with a tail longer than a merchant ship and a head as high as a tower. There was so much commotion on the ground, but the air was quiet and free.

"Galveo!" I heard Sella call my name. I stood, somewhat dazed by Melody's poem. I unlatched my door. Sella entered and immediately noted Melody, her book. Her face registered disgust, and she pretended not to see my scribe. "Some captain, you are," she said to me. "There is land less than a day away and you hole-up here like an overfed mouse. For the love of John, would you come out and be with your crew!" She flung open my closet, and threw a hat at me. Melody shuddered that Sella was so close to the globe. I was seated on the planked floor and the hat rested on my lap. Its bright plume tickled my bare forearm. "Would you wear it?" she said. I laughed. "It's a Crown captain's hat, and you're about to claim a new island for the state," Sella said.

"Where are your combs, Sella? If I remember right, Trinket pins your hair and puts it in curls," I said. Sella took a deep breath. She brought her long sable braid around so that it rested on her shoulder. She untied it, separating the strands. Melody smiled at me. I was certain that

Night Ship: A Voyage of Discovery

Trinket had never decorated such a flow of hair. There was an odd rightness in having this battle maiden primped with colored beads and golden pins, blushing all the while.

I picked up my hat, staring at it, contemplating wearing it. I looked to Melody. It was every bit as silly as having my hair adorned with crystal. Melody smiled and nodded as a sign of approval. I fixed it on my head and went to the looking-glass for a peek. Why not? It seemed that Sella's fate was far worse, and we were having a party. We went on deck to celebrate.

Trinket swayed from the effects of madeira, circling Sella, who was seated on a stool by the mainsail. Her heavy combs were dotted with polished and colorful glass. Trinket held up a swatch of Sella's hair, giggling as she put in her elaborate designs. Sella's face was determined to go through with the humiliation and showed little distress. But her cup was kept full of the potent drink. Her eyes always accused me in some way of being the bigger fool. Nic huddled near her blacksmith's pit; the fire that had cast marine hardware now grilled fat tuna steaks and baked fresh biscuits and cakes. Nic lit the torches and their light threw shadows, but showed off our sovereign's flags; they were strung around the center deck as if marking the boundaries of a carnival. Mahajan smoked from a ceramic pipe that was shaped like the letter J.

In her broken language, Mahajan told Nic stories of sea monsters that were never caught by sailors, were only seen like morning mists before they disappeared. Nic was far too practical for Mahajan's tales and listened with a cynic's ear. But she inquired about the stories' details, which stirred Mahajan's imagination even further.

Mahajan told Nic that she was born of Indian royalty, that her mother was a princess and her father was a common sailor. But as a child, Mahajan herself, had been married to a fine prince who owned seven palaces; each one was landscaped with evergreen trees that bloomed with chalky and faintly blue berries. I could tell that Nic didn't know whether to sneer or to smile with delight at the report.

"What color was his hair?" she said, to let Mahajan know that she was no gullible listener who would take general ideas for truth. Melody stood beside me, tuning her violin. Sella put her hands on her ears, and sighed. Trinket slapped Sella's shoulder as if to tell her to sit still and in place. Nic growled at Melody; my mechanic could not fathom the usefulness of a scribe on a Night Ship. Mahajan lit her pipe with a flaming twig and settled back as if her lies had won out for now.

"Go on and play," I said. I stood, woozy from my portion of the wine. I put my hand out to Trinket. She smiled at my hat, took my hand, and left Sella with half her hair up and half her hair down. The music was quick and joyful. I danced around the deck with Trinket. Trinket laughed and her happiness now brought a grin to Nic's face. Foolish behavior spread like the measles. Nic began to hum and then to sing. Her voice was gay and loud. Mahajan stood, stepped forward and back, all the while letting out puffs of smoke. She watched her feet and their movement. She stooped down and rose, going forward and back. I let Trinket free. She extended both her arms to the sky and danced off by herself, as if her partner were the moon, the stars looking on at their merriment. I went to Sella and offered her a dance.

"Nitwit," she said. I felt my weight teeter. I threw up my hands and backed up to Mahajan. We went round and round the pit. I twirled. She twirled. We stooped and rose, kicked high and low. Melody played faster and my breath was short. I pulled in some air and swayed back to Sella.

"Dance, Sella," I said.

"I don't," she said. "I don't dance, Galveo." I pulled her to her feet, and when she stood, it sured my footing.

"For the love of John, Sella, move yourself," I said. I felt as if I were pushing an unwilling tree and then finally her movement became easy, and I led her around the pit for the rest of the song. Sella's unfinished hair made her appear as if she had two faces, one as dignified and noble as a queen at Court and the other as unknowing as a shepherd girl.

"You've had your fun, Galveo." Sella looked for Trinket and then began to remove the golden pins from her hair. The fire was now dim, and my crew seemed infinitely human and friendly. Even Sella had danced to Melody's music. I felt like I should call my scribe and write down the event; it fascinated me that the brilliant navigator was so afraid to play.

"Won't you make a speech?"

"A speech?"

"History isn't made everyday, Galveo. Why, you act like you've only found a clam shell," said Sella.

"I take no credit for this find," I said. My tone was suddenly grave. "It was not my doing."

"Whose glory then, Galveo?"

"Not mine," I said.

"Your humility turns my stomach. The good and great Galveo!" Sella laughed. "Always giving credit to someone else. Always grateful. Always, always humble!"

"I don't know that my goodness has anything to do with finding the island that so pleases you," I said.

"What else, then? Surely, it couldn't be your simple intelligence. You'd not see yourself as so mystically favored if you claimed your wit. You won't show me your figures, so certainly it's your goodness. It pleases you also that your goodness is far better than your math."

"I have a gift," I said. Melody overheard my words and spilled her madeira onto my lap. She bent down to mop up the wine, and her eyes warned me not to share the globe.

"Of course, you've a gift, you idiot. So spare me your humility," Sella said. "Tell me no more." Sella stood, walked to Trinket's bucket of ornaments and dropped in her loose pins. She turned back to me, and fixed her gaze on my feathered cap. Then she shook her head in a mocking way and was gone.

Sella

The taxi drove down Lake Shore Drive, past downtown. I looked out the back seat window as we moved away from the hotel. The driver came to a light, and honked at the car in front of us when the signal turned green. A wrapped box was set on my lap, and I wondered what was in store for me when the cab came to the end of its fare. It had been a long time since I'd been in the old neighborhood and seen its shabby houses, the small businesses that went up between the buildings, the bars, the massage parlors. It had been a long time since I'd been home.

I snuggled into my cashmere coat, as if the material covering my skirt was the best real me. What happened to the other me, for surely it was another person who grew up in that setting? My story was like the one about the prince and the pauper; and I turned out to be royalty after all. The other Sella Brian disappeared, was lost at sea, was put out of action, or simply never came home one night after working a double shift at Denny's. Actually, she faded away at Harvard University.

"Lady?" the cabbie said.

"Yes," I said.

"Lady, do you know where you're going in this town? I just want to make sure because it's not so nice, this address. It's rough where you're going."

"Yes," I said quickly as if what the man asked was really none of his business. He was probably a boy scout once. The driver cut through the traffic, switched to one lane, and then back. It was better than in the old days. When I was young and took taxis, I'd have them let me out two miles from my home. Two miles away, the neighborhood was only borderline trashy.

The city still gave the residents free trash cans, but there were actual houses, with trees, and driveways. I laughed to myself, remembering that I used to think a poured cement driveway was a status symbol. For one thing, it meant that your family owned a car that could be packed up and taken on a vacation.

The driver stopped, leaned his elbow over the front seat and looked back to me, waiting for his money. I flipped open my purse and gave him twenty dollars. He looked at my legs and winked. I looked at the toothpick hanging out of his mouth. He probably shacked up with his children's mother, probably refused to marry her. I searched the door for a way to get out, fumbling with my package.

He leered at me, was greatly amused that his gesture bothered me. "I wouldn't stay around here after dark," he said. I wanted to tell him that I'd been in this neighborhood after dark for most of my childhood.

"Thanks," I said. I slammed the door. My purse was in one hand and my gift was in the other. I began walking down the broken sidewalk; its concrete was rough and had fixed pieces of stones; chips of green glass were on its surface. The surface caved in at places, giving way to the dirt. I lifted my gaze. I was approaching a gang of boys that swaggered as a group. They crossed each other's paths, bumped into each other, and then separated. The boys spotted me.

"You're so pretty. You're so pretty." They sang a song from "Westside Story." They came closer to me. I looked straight ahead. I had learned never to look away in these situations.

"Go back to Northbrook," one boy said to me as they went by. I turned up to the steps of a brick building. The door was heavy and painted gold. I pressed down hard on its brass handle and pushed it open until I was in a foyer. I ran up the steps, came to a door numbered 8. I knocked on the door. "Mama?" I said. Mama came to the door in an aqua cotton robe.

"Hi," Mama said. Her eyes ran down my coat and to my shoes. She walked away from the opened door, expecting that I would follow her to the couch. Mama had been watching television. A little Christmas tree was on the coffee table, and there was an empty Pepsi can under it. Mama was using it for an ashtray. She sat down and pulled in her cigarette pack so that it was closer to her. She looked at my gift, and then lit one of her Winstons.

"How's I to know that you'd pop in on Christmas Eve," Mama said. "I'm sorry you brought a present. I don't have anything for you. Haven't been out and didn't know you were coming."

"That's okay. It's good to see you. You look good," I said. Mama looked away as if she didn't believe me.

"Where's Steve?" Mama said.

"He stayed behind at the hotel. He had some work to do," I said. Mama exhaled smoke forcefully as if somehow that action replied to me. She tapped the cigarette's red coal on the can's opening.

"You two are pretty fancy," she said. What, you're some kind of computer person now?"

"Yes." "Pretty fancy," she said again. "I suppose I'd better put on my manners and offer you something." Mama laughed softly and dropped the spent cigarette into the can.

"No, I don't want anything."

"No, I suppose not. I've a cold Pepsi in the fridge. Well if you don't want it, don't mind if I do." She picked up her empty can and walked into the kitchen. "Not much new happening. I manage to get by on Social Security, and I play Bingo down at St. Joe's every week." She paused. "Won seventy bucks a week or two ago. Look, I have some crackers if you want some."

"No, Mama."

Mama turned up the television and settled back onto the couch. "Ever watch this show?" she said. "I usually don't like game shows, but this one takes some smarts. Oh, not the same kind of smarts you have, for sure."

"I've never seen it. I've heard about it, though," I said, hoping not to close down the conversation. "Here Mama, open your present!" I slid the gift over to her. Mama set her soda can down. Her head dropped slightly and her fingers tore at the corner of the gift's wrapping. Mama held up a dress woven with crimson and black thread, a classy design. The neckline was simple, with no collar. It was a dress that one might wear to an evening social. Mama brought the dress down to her lap and fooled with the brand tags.

"It's nice, Sella. Next time I go to a party, I'll wear it." She didn't look at me when I told her that I needed to use the bathroom. So I stood and walked up the narrow stairs and stopped for a minute in front of the room that used to be mine. My scholastic ribbons and awards had been taken down. I walked to the window. The view was of roof tops and gutters; gray pigeons gathered along the drain. How many dreams originated in this room? How many plans did I make for getting away from here? The people in my reading led delightful lives, so full of honor. They had nice homes in country settings. They said important things to each other, their conversations were full of wit and color. The people who I read about did something in the world, left their mark on their families and their societies. I wanted more than roof tops and gutters lined with fat birds.

I went to the bathroom and looked at the metal-framed mirror, hiding medicine. I saw every one of my ironed collars, sharp and creased, as a way of making what was old new again. I had studied everyday, and planned a new me. Merit scholarships were my chance to be re-made.

Coming down the steps, I held tight to the painted banister, as if I might fall and never be able to pick myself up again. Fate might turn on me, and leave me stretched out on the tile for eternity. Soda can after soda can would sound from the trash; the night would ring gunshots and angry disputes. Sirens would awaken me at rude hours, and I would be returned to my cocoon like a failed butterfly that couldn't gain flight.

When I returned to the living room, Mama was writing in her checkbook. "Let me give you a little something," she said. "It ain't much, but then you know I don't have much anyhow."

I didn't want Mama's check; it seemed as if she were paying a bill for the dress. "I can't take your money."

She glared at me, and then crammed the check into my hand. "Why not, my money not good enough for you either?" Her face blushed. "You come over here with your fancy-assed dress just to show off all the money you have.

Well Sella, you ain't the only one who can give a present."

"I wanted you to have the dress," I said.

"Sella!" she said. "If I wore that dress around here, they'd arrest me for who knows what!"

"Call me a cab," I said, fighting back tears. I wasn't going to cry in front of her now. I grabbed back the package; torn wrapping paper was still hanging off the sides of the box.

"Mama," I said.

Mother brought the soda can up to her lips and walked to the phone. She dialed, turned away from me. "My daughter needs a taxi," she said into the receiver. She paced in circles until the cord was wrapped around her waist. "Damn, this thing." She pushed it down so that she could step out of it. I decided to leave and call her on another day, maybe after I returned to Boston.

I dropped the package on the floor and went to stand on the outside steps, waiting for my cab.

On Lake Shore Drive near the hotel, there was a sidewalk that ran along the lake. Lake Michigan's waves pounded hard against the shore. "Let me out. This is far enough." The driver turned his head. "This is far enough!"

I said again. I planned to walk along the lake. Navigation lights blinked red and green in the distance as if somehow they knew that it was Christmas Eve. That night I dreamed of being on a ship that had a good captain.

"Galveo, this is your island." I held the map down with the length of my arms. The captain studied my chart, then put her hand up to her forehead and moved away her rusty brown hair. Her finger traced around the island's boundaries.

"Your drawing is wonderful. I doubt that there is a better map-maker under the Crown," Galveo said.

"Those are our maps," I said pointing to a barrel of scrolls. "I'm sure that nothing but honor awaits you, Galveo. No captain has ever been so successful at finding new lands." Galveo wasn't fond of praise for her land acquisitions. That was the curious thing about her. Yet I might have flattered her simply to hear her kind words. She always gave them back to me.

There was no doubt that the captain had won my honest admiration. My doubts about her soon passed away. Her rudder settings, however

Night Ship: A Voyage of Discovery

determined, found islands again and again. The ship was stocked full with fresh fruit and traded goods. It was a bounty that I'd only known on the Night Ship. On the ship, the flour never went wormy. Our sailors seldom became sick from a lack of greens. Galveo's good fortune quickly became our own. I felt certain that we would find a Western route to the East Indies in no time.

I no longer argued about Galveo's math. Her manner advised the crew that no good came from quarrels. I watched Galveo now. For I was convinced that her great gift had nothing to do with her ability to chart from the stars. Whatever was in her heart, I wanted.

Melody came to my office, looking for the captain. Her eyes assessed my awards for navigation. They ran up and down my cabin's walls, noting my citations from the king. Scribes believed themselves to be blessed with huge wit; they knew language when few others wrote their own names.

"Melody," I said in front of the captain. "I'd like to sit in when you read your poems to Galveo."

Galveo smiled at my latest attempt at reform. "That sounds like a grand idea, Sella." Melody scowled at me; she secretly hated sharing Galveo. She enjoyed her position as a tutor to the captain. But a captain needed a navigator and a map-maker, not a reader of poetry.

"Do join us," Melody said. Melody tugged at the captain's sleeve like a child at the market.

"Will you come with us, Sella?" Galveo said.

"Yes, Galveo. I'll come along as soon as I put away my pens and drawings. I rolled the map on my table, tightly and quickly. I rose and took the captain by the arm, nudging Melody into the hard doorway.

Mahajan cornered Nic. Her lips formed the letter O as if she were telling a tale with an amazing ending. "Mahajan," I called down the deck. Mahajan still cowered at seeing me. I walked up to the chubby Indian woman. "Perhaps Melody here can teach you how to write your stories down!" The Indian woman nodded her head as if the idea gave her pleasure.

Melody fell behind the captain and me. She came into Galveo's cabin and seemed very perturbed that I was sitting in on her lesson.

Galveo took her place on the floor, so I did too. I leaned close to the captain and this pleased me. Galveo shut her eyes, and Melody began to read aloud. I decided that I would just watch the scribe form her words. It was a talent that I could acquire if I put my mind to it.

I didn't think much of verse. The lying Indian woman was as interesting as anything that Melody read. Galveo was enchanted by this activity, though. She looked as if she were sleeping, but opened an eye to me every now and then. She tapped her foot to the scribe's voice. I stood, took a lemon from the captain's bowl and cut it with my small knife.

I put a segment near the captain's lips. She puckered and frowned at the taste; then she held the segment with her own hand. Melody warned me with her eyes; she looked like a schoolmistress. When she turned the page, I applauded loudly. The captain opened her eye again. Melody finished the poem and left us.

"Galveo," what do you think when she reads?"

"I don't think, I see," she said. "I see buds breaking through thin snow. I see mother birds building nests." Galveo imagined places that she had never been before, that was part of her gift for finding land. "You don't take it seriously enough, Sella." I took Melody's book from the captain's table.

"Shut your eyes, Galveo," I said. "I'm going to read." I read a few stanzas, heard the sounds. I closed the book and moved closer to the captain. I rested against her arm and felt safe.

"What did you see?" I said. "Giant turtles," said Galveo.

"Turtles?" I looked at her. Galveo began to smile. She stood, opened the door of her cabin. The wind was whipping the sails and seemed to be coming from every direction. I walked onto the deck. Galveo looked concerned. A spray went over the bow. The captain walked away from me, looking for Nic.

Trinket was playing with her goats, buzzing around them like a bee, keeping them together as a herd. "Take them below!" I said. "Can't you see that there's a storm?" She smiled at me, begging my patience. She knelt down to one goat and whispered to it as if she were telling it a secret.

"Move the blasted creatures!" I walked to her and took the prod that she carried like a wand. She stood and grabbed it back from me. Her round blue eyes were defiant. She stooped and spoke childishly to the animal.

"Don't talk to goats," I said.

"Sella," she said. "Sella, just look at their eyes. How can you be so rude to them?" I employed a different strategy. I bent down and lifted the muzzle of the goat. I looked deeply into its green eyes. It did have a gentle, half scared look about it. My recognition of that quality surprised me. Had I gone simple? Did an association with simpletons do one in?

I sighed, giving in to my kindness. No one was looking but Trinket. I stroked the goat and felt its coarse coat. The possibility occurred to me that one didn't have to be dumb to love these animals. I pulled my hand away. The thought stayed in my mind. "Please take them off deck," I said.

"Won't you come with us, Sella?" Trinket said.

I shook my head. "No, I've things to do." I felt blood rushing to my face. I wanted to get away, forget the whole foolish scene. I let mathematical calculations run through my mind as if to reengage my brain. Still my hand went down to the animal, and I was petting it. Trinket smiled at me.

"Take them off," I said. I turned quickly and looked for Galveo. The clouds were like a great wall on the horizon. The wind caught my blouse and inflated it like it was a mainsail. The next I knew I was stretched out in Galveo's bunk. Nic was beside me, offering me warm soup. A pulley wheel had come down on my head, leaving a huge gash on my forehead. While I was unconscious, Nic had wrapped my head in a turban-like dressing. My eyes were nearly covered by the cloth. What explained Nic's gentle nursing skills? In my delusional state, I imagined that I had been mistaken for the Indian woman. Galveo came in to see about my condition, if it had changed.

She excused Nic to check on the sails. She quietly sat beside me, and I felt certain that I could sleep in her presence. No more harm could come to me with Galveo by my side. The ship rocked as in a mother's arms. Galveo's unbolted door swung open from a gust of wind and banged against the cabin wall. Yet the noise did not bother me. I was too sick and too tired.

The Indian woman did the next watch. What accounted for her willingness to care for me? The bandage's edge blurred my vision and reminded me of my headdress. Mahajan may have taken me for an invalid kinswoman. The lure of the turban was too strong for a native! The sight of her gave me fantastic dreams; I was a dancer at a Spanish bullfight. I enamored the crowd with my light feet, and they roared with approval, begged me for a spirited encore.

I wore a red dress, with black sequins sewn on its ruffle. The men smiled, the women envied my beauty. The crowd threw me kisses and long-stemmed flowers. The blooms surrounded my feet. Then the stands were empty. Their silence awakened me. I was now looking at the Indian woman. She smiled, showing her white teeth, and her mouth was like the letter U.

I grew better as the days passed. Galveo walked me onto the deck, holding onto my arm as if I were elderly. She escorted me to the bow, insisting that the air would improve my health. Galveo took me back to the helm and sat me in front of Mahajan to keep me company while she did her duties around the ship. The woman steered the vessel and told me how she came to Night Ship.

It seemed that the native was the last surviving member of a trading ship; the crew fell from illness. On the silent deck, Mahajan saw the billowing sails of another vessel. She swam for seventy-two hours in the choppy seas, floating and bobbing, riding on the back of a blue whale. Still the ship pulled away from her, and she lost all hope of ever seeing her family again. Galveo came along and retrieved her from the ocean.

Galveo and Nic were preparing to explore our latest find. They fooled with the landing boat's ropes. Trinket was nearby, waiting to pack her cheap necklaces and mirrors onto the craft.

Melody's hair was blowing straight out as if it were a windsock. She held the ship's journal close to her. I was determined to go along on this expedition. I was beginning to feel that I was no use on the voyage. The small boat was stuffed full of trading goods; the crew boarded. Nic lowered us with the ropes onto the sea. The oar's handles stuck out like elbows.

Mahajan sat on the rim of the craft's bow, and we hadn't rowed far before she toppled from her seat into the waves. I expected to see a Herculean stroke from the native.

"Help!" she cried and went under. Her black hair looked like a wet feather duster. She gasped for air.

"The damned lying fool," I said. "She can't swim!" Galveo went over the side to pull Mahajan from the water. Mahajan pushed Galveo's head under and used the captain like a ladder, climbing up her body, causing her to sink.

"No!" Galveo yelled at her. It looked as if the drowning woman would drown the captain as well. Galveo wrestled with her. Mahajan scratched at Galveo's face. Her arms beat at the water, occasionally striking the captain.

I looked at Melody. She was stiff with an expression of horror. Trinket was on the craft's floor, hiding. Nic was turning the boat with her oars, going around and around. I pulled an oar up from the lock and swung the heavy lumber into Mahajan's jaw. She fell back, letting loose of the captain. Galveo pulled her in with her arm, and secured her by the neck.

Once in the boat, the tubby helmswoman rested against our trading chests. She drew in air frantically. Galveo's face was marked by fingernails. I looked at Mahajan. "How did you ever get on a ship?"

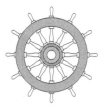

Mahajan

Mrs. Loomsley was closing down the restaurant early on account of it being Christmas Eve. Mrs. Loomsley was the American friend of my uncle "Harry." Harry was not his real name, but he chose Harry because he thought it sounded the most American. My uncle had owned a restaurant too and brought me to America to work in his kitchen. He promised that I could attend a university in Baltimore. But his business failed shortly after I arrived. He didn't have the money for my return to India and so put me in touch with Mrs. Loomsley. I washed pots and pans in her restaurant. My hands waded through thick soapy water, and I dreamed of going home.

The restaurant served a turkey special for lunch. Mrs. Loomsley made a plate for me to take back to my apartment. The lady felt sorry for me, alone, on a holiday. I was so far away from my parents and so young. She told me that. Her face wrinkled like it was pained. When she expressed her worry and sympathy, I told her that I wanted to stay in America, that I really had the means to go home; my father was a brilliant surgeon in Bombay. (My father actually sold insurance and with his small income could never send enough money in dollars for me to board a plane.) It was a degrading thing to receive so much pity from an American.

It seemed to me that Americans loved to pity. Mrs. Loomsley poured me milk from a plastic carton. She had read an article about India; the magazine showed cows walking through the streets of our cities. She wondered about how we came by fresh milk if cows were so free to roam. I told her that we seldom drank milk because sparkling champagne was the drink of choice with meals.

"At every meal?" she asked.

"Not with the morning meal," I told her.

I think that Mrs. Loomsley was a kind lady but not very smart. The turkey platter was an example. I didn't like mashed potatoes. There was no food more bland. The cook boiled some old potatoes and then smashed them, then put a dab of turkey drippings on them. Poor Mrs. Loomsley gave me these so I wouldn't feel so very homesick!

Now I had a toothache, and Mrs. Loomsley made arrangements for me to go to a dentist at the free clinic. The clinic was only open during the morning hours; the dentists also left early because of Christmas Eve. Mrs. Loomsley gave me bus money and detailed instructions about my stops.

"Leave these," she said. She pointed to the dirty pots in my washing tub. I dried my hands and took my turkey platter down from a stainless warming shelf. "You won't be lonely?"

"I have many American friends," I told her. "They've invited me to a party tonight. They'll have a great fat man dressed up as a Santa Claus. They've one that pretends to be Frosty the

Snowman. There'll be many presents for me to open, all very bright and colorful."

Mrs. Loomsley looked pained again. "Okay," she said. "But do call me if you need anything." She looked at my lunch platter. "You have your instructions about how to get to the dentist's office?"

I nodded. Mrs. Loomsley wondered about my life in America, always wanted to know about my comings and goings. I told her what I wanted her to know, which was very little. She didn't know about Lisa Sophie, a woman who lived in a painted house not far from the restaurant. Lisa Sophie told fortunes by reading the palms of people's hands. The clairvoyant wore a long heavy gown, a spectacle of color. Around her neck, the gown was deep yellow, almost gold, like a child's picture of the afternoon sun. The gown was red at her breasts, then changed into royal blue at her waist.

Lisa Sophie took a short sketching pencil, and her elegant fingers moved across the paper. First she drew a woman, then a man, finally a girl. She tore the sheet from the pad. "These people are waiting for you," Lisa Sophie said.

How could she know my mother, my father, my sister? After the drawing, I made a point to visit Lisa Sophie as much as I could afford. Soon she didn't charge me anymore but dressed me in a festive gown as well. We shared stories like school girls and drank warm soda around her table.

Mrs. Loomsley told me to hurry, guided me to the exit.

Once on the bus, I stuffed the turkey platter under the seat. My tooth and entire jaw hurt badly as if someone had struck me. The downtown buildings were very high and made the bus route seem unusually straight. The bus hugged the curb and occasionally stopped to pick up passengers. Americans on buses never talked to foreigners because they were afraid that the outsiders wouldn't grasp their chatter. But in truth, there wasn't anybody I wanted to talk to now. My head throbbed from the bad tooth. My stop was coming up; my heart raced a little at the thought of standing up on a nearly empty bus, in front of everybody. But I did stand and went down the few steps into the fresh air and the rain.

The university clinic was a maze of buildings. I walked past several buildings and read their names. Finally I came to the dental building and entered the lobby. A receptionist gave me a form to fill out and told me to be seated. I filled in as much information as I could.

The woman took my form and asked me about my name. She mouthed her words in an exaggerated fashion as if I might not understand her. After a long wait, I was taken into a small room and told to sit in the dental chair.

"So you are from India?" The dentist prodded and poked at my teeth with his instruments.

"You're a long way from home," he said. I winced with pain. He one day hoped to visit my country, he told me. "Have you ever had an x-ray of your mouth?" I shook my head and jiggled his hand. The lights were very bright, and I could see the gloomy day from the window. He exchanged small x-ray squares with his assistant, and then left the room.

I shut my eyes and imagined my home. I was with my mother in our apartment; my sister was sweeping the floor. There were portraits of my family by the seashore hanging on the wall.

My father wore a silly Western hat, like the one seen in gangster films. My mother was wearing thin white linen. Her smile was full, and she was dipping her foot into the sea. The memory was cut short by the dentist's voice and his returning to the room.

"We're going to pull the tooth. Normally we might suggest a root canal but pulling the tooth will be less expensive and will give you relief today." The dentist paused. "It's best probably if we put you out."

I settled back into the chair and tried to ignore my rescuers, tried to recapture the vacation scene of many years ago. I would imagine the rocking of the ocean and how it was to be in the company of one's own family, in one's own land. I would no longer think of my tooth or my pain. My imagining, however, put me in the middle of a small boat, where I sat holding my jaw.

"So answer me. How did you ever get on a ship?" Sella asked again.

She glared at me. Her eyes turned to the captain, who was being comforted by Melody.

Sella's blue eyes immediately registered alarm, and she went to Galveo in an instant. Sella pulled back on Melody's shoulder and tried to separate the scribe from the captain.

"Give Galveo room," Sella demanded, and then, having moved Melody away from Galveo, she sunk in closely and rested next to the tired captain. Nic began rowing again.

My breath had returned to me. Trinket kept her eyes fixed upon the island; she was oddly preoccupied by the sight, as if she were about to embark upon a calling of some sort.

Melody was still upset from the incident and from being forcefully removed from Galveo. Her back was turned to us all like she was trying to hide her emotions. It was a good time to tell my story.

"I was hired by my Uncle Hirandra to sail away from India, and he promised a way back."

Sella whispered to Galveo. "More lies," she said.

"My uncle was a wealthy trader and was committed to sharing his gold with family members. His ship had four masts and ample room for sixty sailors. He taught me how to guide the ship from the helm and was never far away from me." Nic smiled at the idea of a ship with four masts.

Melody turned back to the captain every now and then, hoping to catch her eye and perhaps her sympathy, but Galveo's thoughts were absorbed in Sella. Sella guarded Galveo as if she were a rare and coveted museum piece, finely sculpted and made out of the most valuable material.

"Hirandra owned not one ship, but many ships, all with four masts." I waited for the mechanic's reaction to my latest claim. Nic's face brightened with delight and disbelief at the possibility of such a powerful fleet. She raised her brow to me, questioning the facts.

"My story is true," I told her.

"Four masts?" Nic chuckled to herself. "There isn't a ship been built that has four masts!" Nic rowed with new gusto. Her strong arms pulled back and went forward, making the small boat go at a hearty pace toward land. As we approached a landing, I again went over the side but this time the water only reached my waist. The beach felt strangely sturdy. Grains of sand swept over my feet. The island was a mix of sand and timber.

I covered my eyes for never had I seen such extraordinary color. It was as if a painter had brushed a shiny rainbow down on the landscape and the oils were still wet. Green, green trees were full of magnificent scarlet flowers. Orange and blue birds were perched in their boughs.

Trinket was next to leave the landing boat. She listened to the sounds of the island as if she heard distant drums. Sella left Galveo's side and hopped onto the beach, noting its contour. Melody waited for Galveo to rise and then followed her onto the land like a loyal terrier. Galveo stooped and dug her hand into the earth. She smiled at me for steering so well. Then the captain ventured into the island's forests and came back with the news that we would build huts and stay to study its geography. The bananas were a blinding yellow. What accounted for the unusually bright color, hues that seemed to drip with gloss?

In the following days, Nic and I made bricks from the soil. We mixed mud and sand and cut them into blocks to dry in the sun. Melody and

Trinket gathered long limbs and fallen palm leaves for the roofs. Galveo and Sella took extended walks up the coast and drew small maps. Sometimes Melody went along to write down the day's findings. The tension between Sella and Melody grew more intense. Then one day Sella took Melody's journal.

"I will write from now on," Sella advised Melody.

"I was hired on as a scribe. It's my job to record the happenings of the voyage for the Crown of John."

"Nonsense."

"Let Galveo decide," Melody said.

Sella called Galveo to the scene. "Galveo, we've much work to do. I see no reason why Melody has to come along with us on our charting missions simply to write. I'm able to do her duty, and she can busy herself in other ways."

"Melody is my scribe." Galveo smiled pleasantly.

I watched Sella sharply turn her back on Galveo and walk up the long coast by herself. The captain's smile fell, and she went after Sella. Galveo trailed after her for a nearly a mile. Then they finally faced each other. Sella's arms flew up and down as a gesture to whatever she was telling the captain. Galveo returned to Melody by herself and asked to keep the journal.

"Only for a while," Galveo said.

"Anna Galveo, please don't let Sella run you. You'll lose something of yourself." Galveo nodded but refused to look directly at Melody. The captain stood silent for a moment.

"You need to keep a watch on Trinket. She's going off into the woods more and more by herself. Would you do that for me? Trinket worries too little about the beasts of the forest." Galveo was obviously drained by the drama. Her face was drawn and weary.

Melody looked down the shore at the sulking Sella. "You're my captain, and I'll do what you want."

Nic grumbled to me. "Of course Melody watches Trinket! We must build the huts by ourselves. What a crew this is!" Nic stacked block after block. "Idle hands," Nic said as the captain passed by.

Nic wasn't interested in Uncle Hirandra anymore and wanted to speak only about the captain and Sella. It wasn't like Galveo to relieve Melody of her job. Melody and the captain were very close. Nic crossed her fingers tightly to illustrate the point. Sella had finally made Galveo give up her good sense, she seemed to be saying.

I told Nic about my evening hours at the helm. Galveo and Sella would stand at the bow for hours. They had a false impression of privacy and didn't know that the shining moon gave them away. "They'd talk and carry on like there was nobody else in the world," I said.

"What do you mean? Did they touch?" Nic stacked bricks, but her mind was intent on my tale.

"Touch? They were like crossing vines. Galveo couldn't let her go. And you know how Sella is." Nic's expression reacted to the thought of Sella holding the captain. I could tell that she thought it would be better to be caught in the jaws of a crocodile than to know Sella's loving arms.

The huts were finished and were built in a circle. A fire pit was in the center of the construction. The crew gathered in the evenings and discussed observations about the island. They discussed plans for future work, the possibility of putting in a garden for fresh herbs. Melody noted that Trinket was still wandering off into the forest by herself. Nic was determined that Galveo and Sella should be split and so requested Sella's help on every occasion. Nic told Galveo that she needed Sella's opinions on projects; Sella was the brains on the ship. Nic's steady demand for Sella flattered Galveo, and Galveo left Sella behind as a service to us. The mechanic worked Sella like a young pack horse at these times. So when Nic's tools came up missing, she immediately suspected Sella's spite and went to confront her.

"My saw," Nic said. "And my hammer." She came very close to Sella as if she were going to punch her. Galveo stepped in between the two crew members. "Sellaaa, give me back my tools!" Nic yelled.

"I don't have your damned tools," Sella laughed. She smiled. "The fool's been in the sun too long."

Melody came up to the captain and announced that Trinket was also missing, had been gone since morning, and hadn't returned to tend to her goats or to eat her midday meal. I thought I might tell a story about a kidnapped sailor, but nobody was in the mood at the moment. Sella quickly brought out her short maps of the island. Galveo assigned search parties. We had just made our search plans when out of the forest came thirteen natives.

Some of the islanders were tall, and these people accentuated the shortness of the others. They walked toward us in an uneven line. They had complex and colorful designs drawn upon their faces.

Galveo went forward by herself. I heard her explain that she was the captain of Night Ship. I took out my pipe and assessed the situation. Smoke billowed from my pipe's bowl. The tobacco was rich and filled the camp area with a cherry aroma. I made every effort to be calm and took a seemingly aimless walk to the trading chests. Once there, I adorned my neck with strings of glass beads. I quickly fastened combs in my hair and brought out a mirror. I jangled a set of bells. The natives quickly left Galveo, and they came to look into my box.

I did not try to speak with them. I only presented each with a necklace. It came to me that I should laugh aloud and smile when the islanders tried on their baubles. Gaiety was a universal language.

I took my pipe and demonstrated its pleasing qualities. My lips formed a circle; one after another, smoke rings floated in the air. I poked my finger through one ring's center, then through the next.

I watched them blow rings, and they looked like kissing fish. I took my pipe back and took a deep breath. I held the pipe in my teeth and made finger horns at the sides of my head. I let the smoke out of my nose, pretending that I was a mad bull. I offered the pipe back to a particularly amused native. Sella rushed beside me, tired of the games.

The jolly native gave my pipe to Sella, but her head turned quickly as if she were looking for a place to toss the smoking bowl. Her arm made a throwing motion then suddenly stopped. The navigator smiled at the native. She brought the pipe half up to her lips.

"Me?" she said. "You want me to smoke?" Sella said. Her eyes were determined to go along. She looked at me and then at Galveo. The navigator put the pipe's stem in her mouth and drew in a breath. Her face turned as red as a morning sky; then Sella bent over, twirled and coughed and gagged. The islanders laughed at Sella's presumed playfulness. They spoke among themselves, and looked as if they were debating who might try the navigator's stunt. "We're missing a member of our party," Sella said to them.

"Some of our tools are missing too," Nic chimed in.

"The tools," Sella said. "Oh, you may have the tools." Sella shot a look at my friend and accused her of being an idiot. "But we're missing a yellow-headed woman, and we really must have her." Sella's attention was directed at the trading chest. "These things belong to her. They are Trinket's. But I'm sure that she'd be willing to give them to you in a minute." She paused. "You may have these things, but we need to find our missing woman."

Two natives came close to Sella and began assessing her braid. They held it up as if it were a part the goods in our trading chest. I could see that they were measuring it like it were a rope. Then one native removed a knife from an ankle belt, and was about to cut it. Sella turned on her heels and slapped the native hard on the face. She batted away the knife. The assaulted islander was stunned, but the others moved quickly, in pairs, to seize us.

The islanders tied us to trees growing beside the camp with strong twine. They went through our huts and dumped the contents of the trading chests out into the dirt. Crown maps had been rolled into cylinders, and the natives sang into them, and were pleased by the amplified sound. They paged through the ship's journal and then discarded it onto a trash heap. Finally they returned to Sella and her long black braid. The navigator spat at them.

Galveo wrestled with the knot binding her hands; a sturdy weave wore into her wrists as she struggled to free herself. "Let them have your hair," Galveo yelled across the camp to Sella. Sella cursed.

"I'll not." Sella said. She bit one native, and the islander howled like a mournful dog. The natives now surrounded Sella, and one lowered a blade to the back of her head. "Damn you," she screamed.

The islanders turned and faced the forest. Trinket walked onto the unhappy scene with several large cats on goat leashes. She mumbled to them and was unaware of the natives' threat. They watched her smooth the center cat's tawny fur; she giggled when the lion roared and showed its teeth. She carried a stick in one hand, and when she raised it above her head, the cats stood on their hind legs; they danced in a circle around their tamer and were a gentle troupe.

At once, the thirteen natives dropped to their knees. They had never seen tender lions, and they revered the woman who tamed them. They thought it possible that all the members of our party possessed a special charm, a way that transformed a beast's temperament into that of a lamb's. The threatening islander, the native who had eyes for Sella's braid untied her and withstood her curses. Sella snatched the knife away from him to free us.

Trinket was sad about the trading chests and cried about the loss. The islanders, witnessing her grief, dutifully returned every object. As a sign of their remorse, they made wreaths out of berry plants. Melody rushed to Trinket's side, folding her into a soothing embrace.

Sella wanted to think that the supply officer's timely entry was a well-calculated plan. She patted Trinket on the back. Sella spied Galveo and was still miffed about the captain's suggestion that her braid could be handed over as if it were an ornament.

"Give them my hair!" Sella said. Galveo smiled.

Nic complained about her missing tools.

"Shut up about your tools. What a numbskull," Sella told Galveo. Always the peace-maker, Galveo showed the navigator across the camp. Nic was huffing about Sella's insult; her eyes burned and she muttered threats under her breath. Nic was far too earnest to overlook Sella's careless criticism.

I packed my pipe full of tobacco and mused at the verity of the fantastic story enfolding before my eyes; it was one that needed little embellishment.

Trinket was a celebrity and was taken to the island's queen, into the heart of the islanders' civilization. The queen was draped in fabrics, sheets of many shades of blue. She ordered that a blue flag be raised above the natives' tents. The islanders took note and became relaxed at the signal for peace. The natives followed Trinket and pampered her. It began to rain, and they held wide leaves over her head. They made her toys out of shells and whittled wood. They offered her their gold earrings, and she collected them in a pail.

The queen's name was Iris. She inspected the gentle lions and tried to communicate with Trinket about her ability to tame the beasts. With her hands, she indicated that the island's ferocious animals did not respond to color; they could not be calmed by the color blue.

But Trinket was in her own happy world, was fixed on the islanders' fanfare: she had no time for the queen's interest.

"You really ought to punish your people," Sella told the queen. "They tried to cut my braid."

Her Highness examined Sella's braid, called a small party of native weavers over to study it. The queen showed Sella different patterns for weaves. The queen smiled and seemed to indicate that the natives admired Sella's braiding very much. The islanders brought the queen dark green colored sheets and she changed from blues to greens in an instant. Then she took off her cap and stooped before Sella as if she were asking for a braid also. The island's blue flag was taken down and a green-colored one replaced it. The islanders hugged each other and demonstrated loving feelings. Iris took Sella's hands into hers. The queen then motioned to her people, suggesting that Sella had hands like members of her tribe.

"I am a Crown navigator, not a primper of hair," Sella said proudly. But she began to braid the sovereign's locks with the most delicate action.

After Sella finished with the queen's hair, red sheets were placed at her feet. She sent up the red signal and the natives disappeared. Her Highness led our group to the natives' workplace. There were great pots of dyes: blue, green, red, yellow. There were spinners and weavers in rows. When the queen passed in her red robes, the natives' movement and labor increased.

The sovereign explained the caldrons by pointing to the bales of white fabric. The pure material was soaked in the pots and then hung up to dry on lines that extended far past the woods' clearing. Sella followed the lines, then ran back to Galveo. "Galveo, imagine what price the weave would command at a marketplace on the continent! We must have an agreement." Galveo nodded, intrigued by the prospect of trading with the islanders.

The queen noticed the color of my skin. I tried to explain to her that I was a long way from home.

"I'm from India," I said.

The queen took a stick and drew a picture of a woman, then a man, and finally a girl in the soft dirt. She called for her yellow robes and motioned that we should sit together. She stroked my cheek and sang a quiet lullaby. The queen held me in her arms, and I wasn't so homesick. At the sight of the yellow flag, the workers went back to their tents and prepared hot meals; they nursed their infants and sat around their families' hearths. The queen comforted me as if I were an orphan. She saw to it that I was dressed in her same garb like I were a daughter, and it wasn't long before I understood the natives' visual language. While they did speak about particular events and shared knowledge, general emotions were conveyed with color; blues suggested tranquility; greens hinted at desires; red resulted in agitation and industry; still yellow spread a wave of domesticity over the camps.

Trinket made friends with a native named Rawhoo and the two bathed together in a small pond at the center of the island. The watering hole was surrounded by trees and their green hue reflected on its surface. Everyday Trinket combed out Rawhoo's fuzzy and tangled hair while the native sat on a stump. She cooed into the islander's ear and hummed to the tune of the swaying branches. At noon, the sun broke through the shady nook, and the tropical heat compelled the companions to return to their place among the water lilies.

Rawhoo squished mud between her toes and made Trinket laugh. The friends pressed their footprints into the sides of the bank and carved out faces with their feet. Rawhoo was the islanders' apothecary; she brewed elixirs out of seeds and fermented leaves, then stored the strong potions in vials. She had a formula not only for sickness but also for enhancing celebrations.

Trinket asked Rawhoo to show the captain the island's land routes. Anna Galveo was pleased for a while, excited about the maps, happy living at camp, but sometimes a distant expression came over her. I suspected that she reacted to the ocean breezes, and these soft winds reminded her of being on the Night Ship. The captain was becoming restless and eager to set sail. It wasn't long before Galveo ordered a return to the ship.

The islanders organized a farewell parade in honor of Trinket; she was carried on their shoulders through the island's paths. The trees were lined with ropes of flowers, scented blooms showing off the most astonishing and vibrant colors. The young natives rattled yellow gourds and clicked together clam shells, while the older islanders beat out marches with their drums.

Trinket was a celebrity, and I wondered how she would adjust to being a sailor again. Nic and I loaded the boat with dyes, oils, fresh fruit, and fabric. We had come to the island with so little and were going away with a bounty of supplies. Melody seemed to dream of her violin. Sella kept an eye out for her exquisite maps, making sure that all were safely packed in the vessel. As for Galveo, she had signed a trade agreement with Iris and kept it in her breast pocket. But Nic was anxious about the ship and what repairs might be needed after a long absence.

"It'll be a mess," Nic said.

Rawhoo noticed Nic's tenseness, her obvious apprehension about the work ahead. The concerned apothecary offered a remedy for Nic's preoccupation and assured her of the brew's relaxing qualities. Rawhoo held out a spoonful, and Nic widely opened her mouth. She doubted Rawhoo's ability and know-how.

That she consented to take the potion was only a sign of her goodwill.

Nic

On Christmas Eve! The trials of being the town newspaper editor never ended, I thought to myself. I should have taken that job in Memphis. At a larger newspaper, if the copy editor called in sick, I could have fired him, and the newspaper would still get out. More and more, I filled in for every Tom, Dick, and Harry who was slack about the office. But on a holiday? These grumblings went through my head, and I resolved to stop them. Complainers. I hated them, and everyone complained about having to do somebody else's work around here.

I was playing Santa Claus tonight, and even Santa Claus had neglected to wrap the presents for my daughter. The publisher should have known that instead of staying around the Christmas hearth and wrapping presents and leaving out carrots for the reindeer, I was at work. I deserved a bonus, a hike in salary for this. I worked sixty hours a week already. This was definitely above and beyond the call of duty. But what did he care? I imagined that the publisher was in France or England with some cutie, sipping wine in a swanky club.

There were rows of empty desks, the computers all shut down. A sports writer with no life was down the hall. I could smell his doughnuts and his burned coffee. Only someone with no life could drink that swill. Were there even any tournaments tonight? Even hockey players were home with their wives.

I put Natalie's toys out on top of my desk. I was going to wrap her presents before my eyes read an inch of copy. Santa Claus wasn't going to be negligent, not Santa or the editor of the Daily Times for that matter. The other employees were drinking eggnog and reporting the year's successes to their relatives. Great! I couldn't find my pager. What if my husband needed help putting the kid to bed; she wouldn't budge or bathe without a word from her mom. What if my own mother's tenuous condition took a turn and we'd need to take her to hospital emergency? What if Sandra was home early tonight from her aunt's and needed me. Sandra was on my mind, was always on my mind these days. She was a kind of work too, always pulling me away from my family. I couldn't get her out of my head.

I lifted the papers and toys, searching for my pager. Of all the damned things to be missing! I couldn't remember taking it off. Perhaps this was the way that middle-aged women began looking at old age. One day, a most valued possession up and became lost. The memory wouldn't recall the details of the missing object. Workers then began to whisper about you, said that you were a fixture, an antique of sorts, and that your mind was a fog.

The sports writer dropped the pager in front of me. "You left this in the kitchen," he said. "Want some coffee? Some doughnuts?" No, but I thanked him and waited for him to leave, to go into another room.

I checked my messages. One: "Nic, would you pick up some cookies for Santa?" I was Santa. I was the grocery delivery person also.

Two: "This is Sis. Mom thinks she's Eleanor Roosevelt tonight. You'd better call me." Another dysfunctional holiday in store. A Christmas never passed without some drama.

Three: "It's Davis Moses. I'm sorry, but I can't come in tonight. I've relatives in from Atlanta, Georgia and can't leave them." Thank you for all the fucking help, Davis. I supposed that since I'd be in the office until a wee hour, my house would be the last house on Santa's route.

Four: "Nic, It's Sandra. Call me."

Five: "Nic, Rick Stoddard. I wish you'd have let me know earlier. I'm on my way out of town. I can't make it." Can't or won't make it? A Merry Christmas to you too, I thought.

I played my messages again. Sandra's voice calmed me down. Sometimes I imagined that we could just take off for a different city with a clean slate. I hadn't made my life choices yet, and we could begin a life together, find a house, have friends, argue about the brand of shampoo that we'd use. Deep down, I knew that someday it would have to end. I needed to stop it. But for now, I didn't have the courage to give her up.

I picked up the telephone receiver and called my older sister. There was festive commotion in the background; my sister entertained her in-laws on Christmas Eve. The family that she had married into had oodles of children in it. My sister had me hang on while she went to a private extension. After a long wait, she returned to the line and seemed out of breath.

Sis filled me in about our mother. Early today, Mom began rambling about the New Deal and her part in formulating the Depression-era public policy. My mother maintained that she was the first to think of the Civilian Conservation Corps. Sis speculated that our mother truly believed that she was the wife of FDR. We had began to doubt mother's mental stability shortly after Thanksgiving, and now it seemed that we were correct. I explained my situation at the office and encouraged Sis to go on with her party. After the gathering, Sis could call Mother's doctor and see about getting medication for her. Sis insisted that she needed me to handle mother as only I could. Why was I the only one who could deal with her? I'd call Sis back when I was finished here. I put the receiver back, looking at the toys and wrapping paper in front of me. I had a change of heart about what should be done first; Santa Claus's chores could be done later. I switched on my computer and got started.

The news took one's mind away from personal calamity. One article told of an effort to bring up lost ships from the coast of North Carolina, a so-called graveyard of the Atlantic. My mind pictured several historical ships breaking the surface of the water after centuries of being at the bottom of the ocean; the article recalled their days of glory. Spirited sailors had left home seeking their fortunes or maybe they left behind fickle lovers who wouldn't commit, and so in a state of despair, they sailed away from them. Pirates, thieves, boarded their vessels in the night and stole their food and tools. Without supplies, the desperate crews tried to catch a strong wind and to avoid the waves outside of North Carolina's shores. The vessels were sunk.

I wondered at the bleakness of their adventures, the ones I had created.

I wanted to call Sandra but fought the idea. A paper needed to get out; Mother was flirting with the looney bin, and I had presents to wrap for Natalie. I had to be sane and set my priorities straight. Responsible people didn't have time for lovers and for carrying on.

I read local stories; the city council voted on funds to buy more salt trucks to fight the Midwestern ice. I went to the state desk, reading about the legislature's approval of a bill to boost tourism. The national news was about "a terrorist" cutting down the presidential Christmas tree. I scrolled up and down, always returning to the story about the ships off the Carolina coast. The wayward sports writer came into my office and told me that he was leaving for the night. I closed up and locked in the news section of the morning edition. I could now begin wrapping my daughter's gifts. My life seemed like a juggling act, a ball was always in the air waiting to be caught.

Sandra's voice came across on my pager, "Nic, call me."

Nic, call me. Nic, call me. Nic, bring home some cookies. Nic, handle Mom. Nic could do it all.

I cut wrapping for a set of pioneer dolls. I put a call into Sis, feeling very certain that her party was over. Mom claimed to have had dinner with Treasury Secretaries Ogden Mills and Andrew Mellon. She had given up on FDR's administration and had gone back to Hoover's. I told Sis that I couldn't come to town until late Christmas day, that she should contact the doctor.

I taped the fold on the last box. Santa Claus was going to be able to make a stop at my house.

I put the receiver to my ear and called Sandra. Did I get her messages? Why hadn't I called her back?

I looked at my pager. "I just now found my pager," I told her. Sandra needed to see me soon. I promised to make time for her after the holidays. My mind recalled my every responsibility. I would see her, but she had to be patient. The holidays were a busy time of the year. I put the phone down, and sighed at her demands. No, it couldn't go on too much longer.

I buttoned my coat, wrapped a wool scarf around my neck. Then I gathered Natalie's presents. I was going to the store to buy cookies and going home to play Santa. Oddly, the ship story wouldn't leave my mind. And when I finally closed my eyes in bed that night, I conjured up a story about sailors in love. I tried my very best to come between them.

I had a bitter taste in my mouth, and I wondered at Rawhoo's concoction. My first thought was to get the crew back to the Night Ship. My arms rowed and rowed. The sun was in my eyes, causing me to squint. A thin sweat mixed with a steady breeze and cooled my face. On the horizon line, I saw my target, the ship bouncing on distant swells. But what was this? Another ship was approaching us. I stopped our small boat and rubbed my eyes. Was it possible I was seeing things? The foreign ship's hull was torn away, a massive and gaping hole marked her starboard side, yet she was coming forward. A blackish dried moss covered her yards. "Galveo," I said. "Do you see what I see?"

"The Night Ship is a majestic sight," Galveo said. The crew looked toward our ship with a shared satisfaction showing on their faces. No one reacted to the severely damaged caravel. I was surely imagining this scene. A ship could not float, would surely be sunken with such a hull. Shivers spread across my back. I closed my eyes hard and then opened them again.

The Indian woman stared back at the island. "Mahajan," I called to her. "Take the oars. I'm feeling oddly and am in need of a rest." The Indian woman moved to the center of our craft and relieved me of my usual chore. I took her place in front, near the boat's V. Still the foreign ship came forward, then turned as if it would put down an anchor beside the Night Ship. Its image shimmered as if it were a mist caught in the sunlight. It seemed to appear and disappear; its reality seemed hinged upon the clouds passing, upon the return of brilliant rays setting down upon her— the vision was not constant.

What would comfort me? What would calm me? "Tell us a story," I said to the Indian woman. The Indian woman puffed out her chest as if a tale might house itself in her lungs, and she were calling it.

"There was once a captain named Jimmy Jack who used to sail these very waters," Mahajan said.

"Jimmy Jack," Sella snorted. "Captain Jack was an outlaw and a fool." But Galveo knew the sailor, and her memories came back to her. Our captain was silent and wanting to hear what the Indian woman would say about her dear and lost friend.

"What do you know of Jimmy?" Galveo said.

"Jimmy was a captain of a sovereign's vessel. His arms were as strong and as round as a mainmast. He was jolly and played games with his crew during times of doldrums. He carried a small bouncing ball in his shirt and entreated his men to learn how to pick up a varying number of objects while the ball was in the air on a single bounce, then the ball was caught."

"For the love of John," Sella scowled. "He was a traitor."

"No, go on," Galveo instructed the Indian woman.

"Jimmy Jack was an honest gamester and was also known for his ability with darts and pitching coins," Mahajan said.

"So what happened to Jimmy Jack?" I said. I kept my eye on the foreign ship and its wavering image.

"The young, handsome captain was chased by greedy pirates for seven months and was finally run ashore onto the rocks. The ship is said to still sail; Jimmy Jack still roams the ocean and has stopped ships simply to play bouncing ball with sailors from the continent."

"Oh please!" Sella objected. Trinket patted Sella's head, and Sella elbowed her in protest.

"What do you know of this unfortunate sailor?" I asked Galveo. Galveo's face blushed.

"Jimmy Jack and I trained together," Galveo recalled. "It is true that no one pitched coins like that man."

"Surely history won't forget!" Sella added.

"He was an amazing captain," Galveo said softly, not wishing to argue about her friend's ability with Sella.

"What did he find?" Sella wouldn't let the topic drop. "Did he name new islands or contribute to our holdings? Why, archives don't care about a captain who fancied bouncing a ball! He had dangerous ideas, was against empire, spoke about everyone's right to autonomy and self-rule. A mental deficient." Galveo smiled weakly, then let Sella's assessment of Jimmy Jack's posterity go unanswered. But Galveo was holding back, and her mum heart might have cut Sella's to the quick if the discussion had gone further.

Mahajan rowed slowly and surely to the Night Ship. The foreign ship bobbed beside our own. No one spied it but me. Jimmy Jack was returned to visit with Galveo. There was no other explanation for the sorry and flickering vessel. A dream? Insanity? The native's potion? No, Jimmy Jack had unfinished business with our captain and brought his ship to hers.

I pulled myself, arm after arm, up the ship's rope and fastened the landing boat to a pulley. Once on the deck, I could fully see Jimmy Jack's caravel. Its boards were black and soft from brine. I could see the ship's bell and its letters spelling "Exemption." Then I saw the good-looking captain standing at his helm, and his smile was brilliant. He wore thick gray tights and a white belted shirt; the belt's buckle was brass. His hair was brown and straight.

I saluted him as a once Crown captain. When my captain finally stood on Night Ship, I walked over to her and told her of the wrecked visitor. Galveo smiled, "Mahajan tells a story, doesn't she?" Jimmy Jack winked at me and brought up a glowing rose from his deck planks. He extended his arm to me, asking for permission to come aboard. I nodded to him.

He followed Galveo to her cabin; the rose's stem was held loosely in his fingers as if it were a bloom that belonged to our captain, and he had to return it. That night Galveo ordered us onto the deck to play games. We tossed coins and bounced a leather ball into an old bucket.

Jimmy Jack studied the bulwark and then rolled his coin; he had mastered the sport and was the ghostly winner. When he was not playing, he stood by Galveo and rested his arm over her shoulders. She seemed not to be consciously aware of him: she couldn't see him but was somehow informed of his spirit; she remained very close to him all the while.

He spoke to her about aborigines. Galveo appeared indifferent about Jimmy Jack's ideas on liberty and only seemed to mind her own ability with a ball. I heard the rebel Jack say, "No exchange but freedom."

"Silly madness," Sella said, and she refused to play, despite Galveo's pleas for her to join in the fun. It seemed as if our captain had regained a former spirit of youthfulness. Sella's best complaints did not deter her from her folly. Galveo laughed and laughed when her coin came to rest inches from the wall. She kissed Trinket on the cheek when her ball set down in the bucket.

Galveo left Sella on the deck that night and returned to her cabin alone. The next morning, I went early to Galveo's quarters for instructions and caught her in a deep slumber. There was an image of a rose beside the islanders' trade agreement. I looked once and saw them: the flower, then the document that bore the Crown's insignia and promised the exchange of mirrors for the natives' weave. I looked away and then back and both the rose and the agreement disappeared. I ran onto the deck. Jimmy Jack's ship was gone, and my head ached from the night air. I now believed that Rawhoo's strong elixir had an adverse effect on my mind: it was an incredible notion that Jimmy Jack had returned to see Galveo.

Our decks were neglected, and I called upon the crew to swab them with wash. The ship was in such a state of disrepair that Galveo assigned crew members to help me with maintenance. Galveo even rolled up her sleeves, took a bucket and brush, and worked to keep the deck planks from rotting. But the captain tripped over a long-handled mop and stumbled into a vat of wood wash.

I took her aside and suggested that she could sew the damaged sails. But her stitches were jagged, sometimes loose, sometimes the knots weren't tied correctly. There was no job that she could set her mind upon. She was not acting at all like a Crown captain.

I asked her to climb to the crow's-nest. Her footing on the ropes was so unsteady that I worried for her well-being. She kept looking down and around. She looked up to the bow and back to the stern. What was she doing? What idea had her mind in such restless state? Then it came to me. Sella walked below and waved to Galveo. Galveo became as sure-footed as a ewe.

The navigator was painting a section of the deck. I came up beside her and left her a bucket of wash.

"Why don't you leave the captain alone?" I said. This matter between them was my business.

"Why don't you go hold your head under water?" Sella pinched her nose as if she were holding her breath. Women like Sella had brought down kingdoms and made silly fools out of sages. Anna Galveo was my closest friend, and I had an obligation to warn her.

Sella had jerry-rigged a clothesline from above the captain's door. I burst through socks and shirts to see the navigator on the other side. Pins were in her hands. Her hair was down, out of its usual tie, and she looked like a peasant washerwoman. "Who told you to put up this line?"

"These are Galveo's," Sella said as if that answer made everything okay. Then she gave me her shark's smile.

I banged on Galveo's cabin door. My wait wasn't long, and Galveo invited me in to talk. Sella followed behind me. She sat on the floor, and began washing her face in a metal basin. She cupped her hands, filling them with water, then splashed it against her skin.

"Must she stay?" I said.

Galveo moved behind her table and sat down. "Does she bother you, Nic?" Galveo was trying to guess the reason for my visit.

"I need to talk to you, Galveo." Galveo was quiet for a moment, then motioned to Sella. Sella stood, gathered her things, and slammed the door.

"What is it, Nic? What can I help you with?" Galveo nervously rubbed the edge of her table as if she were trying to remove a smudge.

"Anna Galveo, you're my friend. We've sailed the world's oceans. We've climbed to the highest yard and fixed sails that only a bird can see."

"We've done a lot." Galveo wanted to get to the point of my visit. "What is it, Nic?"

"I feel that it's my duty to warn you about the navigator," I said.

"Warn me? Warn me about Sella?" Galveo was both taken aback and amused about my concern.

"Forgive me for saying so, but the crew has noticed that you've changed since she's been hanging around. You're not on deck so early, you're not mindful of what needs to be done. Forgive me again, but Galveo, you're filled with thoughts of something else beside the ship."

"That something would be Sella," Galveo said. The captain searched through her papers as if she had misplaced something important, as if something were missing from her table.

"I don't think you see her as the rest of the crew does," I said. "She's rude and rough." Galveo turned her head toward me. "She takes you in, has from the very start. You've favored her," I said. "But I think she's strange, and I think she's trouble for all of us."

"Are you registering an official complaint against me and my navigator?" Galveo's voice was flat.

"Anna Galveo, you're my friend. I speak to you like you're my friend. I mean no disrespect. I just can't stand to see her pull the wool over your eyes again and again. I don't think you know her."

Galveo's voice lowered and it seemed to shake. "I think I know her best. Please be accurate when you speak about who knows who." The captain looked away and then faced me directly. "If the navigator has done something wrong, really wrong, I'd love to hear about it."

"My missing tools," I said.

"I doubt very much that Sella took your tools. But if you've proof, bring me proof. Won't you do that, Nic?" Galveo stepped toward me, rested her hand on my shoulder. Galveo took my hand and held it. She walked me to her cabin door. I suspected that she was upset by my words but valued our friendship as well.

That evening Mahajan was at the helm, and I told her about my visit and my belief that the captain was far, far gone with infatuation. I leaned against the rain barrel and stared at the stars, at the dark night.

"At eleven, every evening, they sit under the wood tarp," Mahajan told me as if to fuel my displeasure. "You could go to the navigator's cabin and search for your tools. You'll need hard evidence to bring Sella down in the captain's view. It's the only way," she said.

I considered the stealthy action. I could enter her locks without breaking them. I was a mechanic. But somehow I doubted that Sella would be foolish enough to keep tools in her cabin. The idea of the captain and the navigator under the wood tarp intrigued me, though; the possibility of a risky deed was firmly planted in my mind, and I decided to go behind the tarp and listen to their exchange.

At eleven, the helmswoman pointed across the deck, and there just below the bow two shadows ducked into a covered space. I imagined that they liked the air from a night cruise, that there was something exciting about being in the open breeze and hidden too. I crouched down low and walked until I could clearly make out their words through the canvas.

"I wish there were more of a moon," Sella told Galveo. "I went to the supply area and bought a ring for you." There was silence. "You can't see it now but slip it onto a finger. Its band is gold because gold is tender, and its stone is the color blue because the sky is blue and promises always to return."

"Thank you," Galveo said. "Thank you so much. The gift is a thoughtful one. I'll cherish it. I've a gift for you, too, something I want to share with you, something I've wanted to share with you for a long time."

"What is it?"

"Would you believe me if I told you it was the world?"

"Don't be silly, Galveo. What is it?"

"It's the Western passage to the East Indies and more," Galveo said.

My foot nudged a log, causing stacked wood to tumble and to crash beside them. They stood up and walked to the sides of the wood tarp. They replaced the logs. I kept perfectly still. My own breath seemed as loud as a bellows. In a few moments, they sat down.

"You've no gift. You just like to tease me," Sella laughed. Galveo let the subject drop.

I backed away from them, returning to Mahajan. "The problem's worse than I've imagined."

I awoke the next morning with a terrible cold. My nose tickled, and I sneezed. My first thought was to go down to the supply area for a remedy.

The supply area was made up of shelves, and they extended to the ceiling. Trinket arranged the ship's goods by her own method, and so it was nearly impossible to find a particular item on one's own. Usually the supply officer could find most anything in minutes; she'd roll her ladder to just the right shelf and bring down my nails or glue. But Trinket had stepped out.

I surveyed the shelves. I spied one that held canisters. I was looking for a strong aromatic leaf balm and possibly some herbs for tea. I pushed the ladder in front of the medical supplies and climbed to a high shelf. I looked at each label, moving jars aside in my search. My arm reached to the back of the shelf, and my hand landed on a cloth full of something hard. The folded material revealed a wooden handle. I rose up on my feet, standing on my toes. My hammer! My saw! My long missing tools were in front of me, only inches from my grasp. My sinuses cleared from my excitement. I breathed so much more easily. I fully unveiled the objects and fastened them to the hooks on my belt. What a find! But there was one piece in the cloth that was not mine. It was a bracelet which had last belonged to Melody.

I could hear Trinket's high voice at the top of the deck. I had only a few minutes before she would come down the stairs. I stuffed Melody's bracelet in my pocket and made my way down the ladder. I gave the ladder a push, and it glided away from in front of the herb shelf.

Goat hooves clicked on the steps. Trinket's yellow hair seemed to light the dim area. "You'll have to wait," she told me. "You're a bad goat, a bad goat!" She scolded the nanny.

"I can come back," I said.

"Come back later," she said. The goats were idle in a line and seemed to await her next move. Trinket was in a gloomy mood, had not adjusted to her common life and job on the Night Ship.

I caught the daylight, and it invigorated me as if I were a successful thief. But I was not a thief, and neither was Sella, for that matter. Sella was absolved of wrong-doing, but she was still wrong for the captain. Would it be so terrible to plant the tools in her cabin if the captain could be spared from her wiles? Galveo wanted proof. Was it wrong to protect a friend by the means that one had at hand?

I passed Melody on the deck. I decided against my false plan. But I wouldn't go so far as to clear Sella's name. I stopped by the ship's railing and dropped the booty overboard. Sella's innocence would be my knowledge. At least, I wouldn't give my captain any further cause to believe in her.

Melody

The hills of Kentucky were even pretty in the winter; the cedars turned a golden brown and the sycamore groves were in between, white, shining bark giving the trees a ghostly but somehow friendly appearance. The gravel on the road was dry. Pale dust formed clouds beside my car door. A pickup truck was ahead of me and suggested a successful day of hunting; the body of a buck deer rested out past its tailgate. These were the images that entertained me as I came close to my childhood home, a frame house on the West Virginia border.

My father was waiting on the steps for me, already dressed for church. His dark suit made him look like a professional, and odds were, if one had to guess, he was one of a kind in the whole area. His black hair was cleanly cut and shaven. He might have been the town's doctor or lawyer. He might have been the church's minister. But Daddy worked at the refinery in Ashland and simply delighted in fine clothes.

Daddy greeted me. "Melody, sweetie." His arms wrapped around me. I hugged him tightly, feeling his sturdy shoulders. He held me out in front of him as if I were a girl and had grown since last we saw each other. His lips pecked my cheek. He repeated the kiss.

"My things," I said.

"We can get them now or bring them in later," Daddy said. The heel of my shoe came off as I walked around the car. I picked up the short stub. My gait was uneven, and I had to laugh at my silly misfortune.

"I'll fix it for you," Daddy said. He took my violin and suitcase from the trunk. "I'm glad you're home. I've been sitting here for an hour, thought maybe you got held up by something and couldn't leave exactly when you said."

"Daddy, I'm slow. You know I'm slow. Isn't that what you used to say. Melody would be late for a parade that she was riding in."

"We're not having a parade today," Daddy said. His dark eyes sparkled and were filled with joy.

"Where's your boy?"

We climbed the steps. "He's not a boy, Daddy." Daddy smiled at me. "Bus is on his way. He called me at noon and said that he was leaving Nashville after he had lunch. I do want you to like him," I said.

"I'm sure he's fine," Daddy said. "You like him, that's what matters. And you say he's a musician."

"Yes."

"Do musicians make good money?"

"No, they don't," I said. My father smiled at my honesty and understood that the subject was closed.

I was in the living room and saw my pictures on the wall. It embarrassed me to be so much the focus of my parents' lives. I supposed that they were my original fans, sure that one day I'd sing on stage. Mother had made my costumes, and Daddy took pictures from every vantage point.

I walked to my piano, let my fingers trail across the keys. I remembered evenings so full of song and laughter. It was a wonder that I could ever leave my home, there was not a place in the world more safe or secure. Daddy walked to the bottom of the stairs and yelled up to my mother.

"Melody is here!" Daddy was impatient. "Melody!" he said, as if Mother were hard of hearing.

Mother rushed down the steps, took one look at me. "Honey, you're pale. You'd better put on some lipstick. Do you have any?"

I nodded.

"Just go right into the restroom and fix yourself," she said.

I shuffled through my bag and put on red. Mother liked red lipstick; it put the most color in your cheeks.

Mother filled the candy dish and arranged the pillows on the couch. "I can't wait to meet Bus. Is there a history behind that name? It's not a regular name. How'd he come to it?"

"His name is Buster," I said. "That's the name his mother gave. Please don't say anything about his name."

"Oh no, it just doesn't seem like a lot of thought went into it." Mother tried not to be concerned about his background. She brought out a bottle of brandy and poured a small amount into a glass. She put it in my hand. "The whole congregation is anxious to hear you sing."

"I'm glad, Mother. I'm looking forward to being a part of the choir."

"You're not just going to be a part of the choir. I told them that you'd be happy to sing a solo."

"You did?" I said.

"Of course."

"What did you tell them I'd sing?"

"Drink honey," Mother said. Mother poured more brandy in my glass. "I told them you'd decide when you got here."

"Oh," I said. "They put that on the program?"

"Honey, you worry too much."

When Bus pulled into the drive, Daddy was waiting for him. Daddy carried his bags into the house, smiling at me. He set Bus's guitar down by my violin. "The band is here," Daddy said.

Bus smiled at me, and oddly, looked like a towering boy in my parents' home.

Mother wanted to know about the clubs we played in. Were they nice places? I explained to her that they were not always the best. My answer disappointed her, and she suggested that Bus should dress for church, but Bus hadn't brought a suit. Mother was surprised and brought out one of my father's. I could feel blood rising to my face.

"That'll be fine," Bus said.

Bus went along with Mother, even though he was a taller man than my father. The suit pants didn't cover his socks. The ill-fitting and borrowed clothes wouldn't be a problem, though, since Bus would be sitting down in a pew. My mother said that. I began to wonder if Christmas Eve was the best time for a first meeting. Traditions gave a family away, let everyone in on its idiosyncrasies.

"You know," Daddy told Bus, "there's not a thing that we wouldn't do for our Melody. I'd give her the world if it were mine to give."

Bus smiled. He looked at my photos on the wall. I should have warned him about my parents. But they were my parents. I loved them, and there wasn't much that one could do about them anyway. Mother would be forever commenting about dress and appearance. Daddy would just always make my men friends nervous. How could it be helped?

Red poinsettias were arranged in rows around the altar. The choir stood aside from the plants and their satin robes were white. The scene was simple, but somehow it was spectacular to me and brought back memories of Christmas. I supposed all people had one holiday scene that replayed the mood of all the others. The crying babies and and the oversized dresses of young girls were familiar, so familiar that I could have been in a drooping frock with a light blue sash.

Mother brought the minister over to meet Bus. She didn't want him to stand and reveal his ankles. My voice rang throughout the church; it seemed to touch the ceiling and the highest square of stained glass. My spirit soared above the Kentucky hills and might have reached heaven.

After the service, Bus and I walked home. The meadow along the road was like an ocean, not like land at all, but like a harbor that met the land, the higher hills. I thought about gifts and love. My own father's love had made me believe that God sent his son as a gift to the world. Did we need love to believe in love? Didn't everyone need someone who would give them the world if the world were theirs to give?

That night Mother made up the couch for Bus with sheets and blankets. I probably should've warned him.

Galveo summoned me to her cabin. I brought my poetry books and hoped to recite verse. Upon my arrival, the captain took the ragged books and set them aside, out of the way.

"I've decided to share the globe with Sella. She's a Crown navigator, and the globe rightfully belongs to the Crown."

"I see," I said.

"Then you no longer object?"

"Is it for me to advise you, Galveo, when you've made up your mind?"

"You had objections," Galveo said.

"I don't wish to hurt you, Galveo."

"Speak your mind. You're my loyal scribe and my most trusted friend. You may speak freely."

"Okay, then. It's been said that the test of a person's character is when he or she is given power. Sella and power are a bad mix. That was the basis of my objection to her having knowledge of the globe."

Galveo lowered her head at my criticism of Sella. "You don't know her as I know her."

"I don't love her as you love her," I said.

Galveo smiled. "I've not told anyone that."

"A storm doesn't announce its coming. The clouds give it away," I said to the captain.

"Does Sella give herself away as well?" The captain was eager for my answer.

"Are you asking me if she loves you, Galveo?" I said. "I know that she guards you, that she cannot stand to have another be near you." I stopped. "I don't know if that is love."

"What would you call it, then? Surely it's love." The captain went to her cabinet and took out the crated globe.

"Do what you like, Galveo. I won't be so foolish to imagine that I can sway you from where your heart has set down. I can only give you my blessing and fine wishes. That's how I can best serve you now." I walked to my books as if to suggest that our talk was near an end. I had meant what I said but also felt sadness, knowing that Galveo wouldn't call for me as much as she had done in the past.

"Please don't submit to me," Galveo said. "I welcome your sure wisdom and your calm head."

"I'll never choose to be your enemy. I know that it hurts you to hear Sella discounted," I said.

"So you'd abuse her and advise me again not to share the 1957 globe?" the captain said.

"No," I said. "It has been Sella's great fortune to find a true heart. I'll not be the one to say that she doesn't deserve the gifts of that love. I do pray that you're equally as fortunate. I ask you one favor," I said. "Don't be alone when you share the globe. Let me attend you," I said.

"Attend me?" Galveo questioned my choice of words. I wondered about them myself.

"Be with you," I said. Galveo smiled. She picked up an iron bar and pried open the crate.

"Tomorrow," the captain said. "I'll give her the prize of globes. A navigator has never known such a fine gift." I watched Galveo and now understood my words. I needed to be with the captain in case something went wrong. Anna Galveo might be devastated by Sella's reaction.

The following day, Trinket pushed a cart of tableware along the side deck to the captain's cabin. The cart squeaked and clattered as its wheels rolled across the planking. The bowls on board bore the king's insignia and were reserved for only the most extraordinary occasions. Galveo had also ordered the ship's few glazed serving dishes and cloth coverings for the table.

"Is it the captain's birthday?" Trinket asked.

I told Trinket that Galveo was having her evening meal with Sella.

"With Sella?" Trinket laughed at the idea of dragging out the ship's best for the navigator. The supply officer moved more lightly now, knowing that nothing very important was happening if Sella were the guest of honor. I could tell that she worried less about the arrangements and about delivering the right goods. She walked along until she came to Galveo's door.

Galveo's table was covered with books and maps. "How am I supposed to make this table?" Trinket whined.

"We'll move the books," I said. I put my hand down on Galveo's papers and was lost for a moment in the idea that these items belonged to the good captain. My hand almost felt warm.

Trinket threw open the captain's cabinet, and there on top of the crate was the globe.

"Oh my," Trinket said. "I never did see so many colors on a globe, pink and orange and blue!"

I shut the door quickly. "The captain's private things," I said. Trinket lowered her lip to me, showing sadness. "I cannot let you go through the captain's private things," I said. My heart raced, but I calmed myself about Trinket's discovery. She did not know the globe's actual value. What harm could she do, anyway? Galveo did not need to be told of the mishap.

"I was just looking for a place to put all the books on her table. Don't blame me for that." Trinket stomped her foot.

"No, no, nobody is accusing you. But we need to get the table made before she comes back from her rounds."

"One, two, three. That's three bowls," Trinket counted on her fingers. Sella and who is the other guest?"

"Me," I said.

"Why you? The captain never asked me for a meal. Trinket get this. Trinket get that," Trinket stomped her foot again. "I want to go to the captain's party!"

"Maybe the captain will have a bigger party soon. You must not be sad. I am only invited to assist her."

"To record?"

"Yes, to help."

Trinket skipped around the cabin at the idea, thinking that helping didn't sound like much fun. She hummed and sang as if she were sauntering through a field of wild columbines.

"Fill the lanterns," I told her.

"You can fill the lanterns," she said. Then her defiance subsided. "I'll fill the lanterns."

We stood back and admired our work.

"Pretty?" Trinket smiled and held a finger to her cheek as she took in the sight.

"Very pretty," I said. I tucked the extra cloths into the bottom of the cart, and we were off.

Galveo grinned, sitting back waiting for Sella to arrive. She had spent most of the afternoon preparing a chowder. Her face was bright and her white shirt was crisp from drying in the sun.

Sella entered, eyed me the way that misers take in a fast-talking knave who is too close to a treasure. Her hair was back, in its braid, and she looked as if she had just returned from an arduous duty. Sella was beautiful somehow, despite her unpleasant manners. "What's this, a Crown celebration?" she asked.

"It's a special occasion," Galveo said. "I'm going to give you the gift that I've spoken about. But first you must try my thick soup." Sella looked at me, wanting me out of the cabin.

"Are we reading verse?" Sella said.

"We could read verse later," Galveo said.

"Galveo, why is she here?" Sella was tired of being polite and wanted an answer from the captain.

"Sella, be patient and you'll understand many things," Galveo said. The captain stood and began dishing out her recipe. There was always a soft fire in Galveo's eyes; but now their light crackled like dry twigs had been set down upon them. Galveo's face was full of light.

Sella was quiet throughout the meal, and I supposed this was her form of brooding. Galveo's conversation was merry and relieved. She approached the subject of the globe.

"Sometime back, almost a year ago, Melody told me about a crate that was buried in the sand. She happened upon it while walking on the beach." Galveo stopped to make sure that Sella was listening. "I asked Nic and Mahajan to unbury the box. They brought it to my cabin."

"Pirates' loot?" Sella said.

"Well, no, but so much more strange and valuable. An unbelievable find," Galveo said. "You've spoke of our good fortune, of our acquisitions for John. The content of the box is responsible," the captain said.

"Lost charts?" Sella asked.

"Not exactly. An incredible find! A globe, Sella." Galveo said. "A globe dated in the future. Several centuries into the future." Galveo paused. "It is a 1957 globe!"

"Don't play with me, Galveo." Sella was becoming angry.

"Melody and I decided that we shouldn't tell other members of the crew until we were certain of its truth." Galveo rose and went to her closet. She set the object in the center of the table.

Sella picked it up, bore her gaze onto its print. "Your rudder settings were determined by this?"

"Indeed."

"You had this all along and only Melody knew of it?"

"Yes!" Galveo was pleased by how well we had kept our tongues.

"The globe's true?" Sella asked.

"Yes." Galveo smiled fully.

Sella stood. "I'll see you hang for this!" She looked at me. "I'll see you hang for this!" she said.

"Sella?" Galveo said.

"I'm a Crown navigator. I work with maps and charts. It should've been turned over to me immediately. It should've been registered right away as a find for the king. You kept it for yourself."

Galveo shook her head. "If I had given it to you, what would you've done with it? Would you not have called it a fraud and hoax? Would you not have called me crazy if I wanted to test its truth?"

"You're the fraud, Galveo."

"Please stop," I told Sella.

"Please stop! Please stop!" Sella mocked me. She faced the captain. "You led me to believe that it was your goodness that caused us to find those lands. I was right at the first. Your goodness is nothing, never found a thing for the Crown. You are a hoax and a fraud. You made me love you, and you were lying to me, laughing at me, keeping a little secret."

"Sella," Galveo said.

"The globe is mine," Sella said. "It's no gift. It is and always has been the property of the Crown."

Galveo watched her leave, the globe still sitting in the center of the table. Galveo paced back and forth until finally the small area confined her. She went outside and grasped the ship's railing, held it tightly, and tried to regain her senses. Finally she sobbed.

"Dear Galveo, give her time," I said. I took Galveo's hand, and we walked along the railing. "She didn't mean what she said. It was said in haste and with the speed of her temper." I unlocked my cabin and showed Galveo to my bunk. "Rest if you like," I said.

I went to a basin and wet a towel, putting the cloth down on her forehead. "Think no more," I said. "The world will look differently after you sleep and when it's a new day." I left Galveo and went to find Sella. Only Sella could take back her words and really comfort the captain. I went past Galveo's still opened door, and the globe was gone!

I went to Sella's quarters and knocked loudly. There was no answer. I ventured up to the bow and spotted the navigator resting against the bulwark. I sat down beside her and noticed her tears. "Go away," Sella said. "Go away, do you hear me?"

"Return the globe," I said. "And take back your words to the captain." Sella stood and began to walk away. "Sella, please!" I said. "You're angry at me because you suppose that the captain's confidence has been mine. But do accuse me! I advised the captain early on not to let you know about the globe."

"Crown captains do not take orders from scribes," Sella said.

"Crown captains listen to their friends. The fault is mine. Galveo almost told you after the first island."

"I've believed in her silly goodness. I believed that her goodness was the cause of our rewards." Sella was full of self-pity and regret.

"There's no reward for goodness but goodness itself. There's no reward for love but love," I told her.

"Go away from me! Your foolish aphorisms!"

"Will you return the globe and take back your words?" I said.

Sella was startled. "I don't have the globe," she said. "Oh dear, where's Galveo? Where's Galveo?" she said through her tears. She stood and left me alone on the bow.

After a moment, I decided to follow her to the captain. Galveo was now in her quarters, and the room was lit by lanterns. Nic and Mahajan were standing off to the side. Sella was in front of Galveo.

"Say that you have the globe, and there's no crime. You're a Crown navigator, and as you've said, the object belongs to John. It's truly yours to watch. But you must say you have it or there's a crime." Galveo had assumed the role of the captain, and was surprisingly stern with Sella.

"I won't say that I have the globe when I don't. If the globe is gone, you must search the ship. Search the ship!" Sella said with urgency. Galveo didn't respond to her words, but stood in her place as if the navigator had said nothing that altered the situation.

"Your denial is a crime," Galveo said again. "Don't make me arrest you. Say that you have it."

"Galveo," Sella said. "There's a ring on your finger. Do you remember why the band is gold?" Galveo turned her back on Sella, and I saw the captain draw in her breath.

"Don't stab my heart and pull me in with your harpoon and line," Galveo said softly.

"It is gold because gold is tender. The stone is blue because the sky is blue and promises always to return," Sella said. She paused. "I do not love your globe. I love you."

"Galveo," I stepped forward. "Trinket saw the globe when we were making the table. She was looking for somewhere to put your books and went to the closet before I could stop her."

Nic joined in. "Galveo, my tools. Trinket stole my tools. I found them in the supply area along with one of Melody's bracelets."

Trinket

"Katrina's Antiques," I said. "Yes, I do have clocks. I have a ship clock. The ship itself is wooden. The sails are a stainless steel. It has three masts, and the clock's put right into the wood. It would be a wonderful Christmas present for anyone who loves the water." The woman paused on the telephone. "I'm getting ready to close, but if you come over right now to see it, I'll keep the shop open." I put down the phone and looked for Chesterfield and Moe. Chesterfield was in the window and seemed to watch the snowflakes fall.

I picked up the tabby. "We'll have to wait for a customer. Moe," I called. Moe was a kitten and wasn't very smart. I bought him at the pound, and he didn't know his own name. I stroked Chesterfield and listened to him purr. "Imagine not buying a present until Christmas Eve," I said. Chesterfield blinked his eyes at me and also thought the woman was foolish.

Moe rolled on his back underneath the china shelf. "Moe, I used to be a great lady. You wouldn't hide from me if you knew me in my dancing days. Katrina Ball was once a name." I now had my two cats in my arms. "You boys want to see me dance? I bet you've never seen anyone dance like me. The whole house stood in applause, wanting me to come back on stage. I suppose you thought that I was always a junk lady. Well no sirs."

I put the cats down together, and they waited for me to do my routine. I walked out onto the stage. "Chesterfield, I'm dancing. Don't you fall asleep on me. Moe, you'd better watch. You see, I'd go like this first." I put my arms out as if I were ready to fly away.

Chesterfield loved to watch me dance. Chesterfield knew a dancer when he saw one. Moe tried to sneak away, walked over to the chest and drawers. I grabbed him and then completed my turn. "A dancer is an athlete," I told him. "There's nothing easy about dancing for a living." I set the rascal back down. "Ungrateful," I told him. "I rescued you from the shelter, and this is how you treat me. You don't believe that I was a principle dancer in a big city company. I danced in New York, you fool. The most important people in Manhattan watched me dance." I stopped. Chesterfield and Moe toyed with each other. They bit at each other's paws. "How's a girl supposed to feel with you two for an audience?"

The snowflakes were big like spent pieces of bathroom soap. I sat down and sighed. I rested my hand on an umbrella stand. I wondered why nobody liked the stand. Maybe nobody knew what it was. I decided that I'd find an umbrella and put it in the stand as a hint. The shopping season had been slow. I waited for every customer this year. What if the woman didn't show up? I dusted the carnival glass pitcher.

Pretty, pretty, glass! Oh, I owned so many pretty things. I wasn't sure if I cared if anybody bought another thing!

"Chesterfield," I said. "We need some music. That's what's wrong. You boys can't imagine me being a dancer because we've no music. I danced Cinderella and Sleeping Beauty. I danced in The Nutcracker. Everyone dances The Nutcracker at Christmas. Chesterfield and Moe! I insist that you stop treating me like an old washed up woman! Music," I said.

I put a record on the player. The player's arm stayed above the swirling disc, so I set it down. "Do you hear the violins? Listen to the percussion. You felines simply have no taste." The bell rang. My customer. My customer had come to look at the ship clock!

"Oh don't mind me. You see I used to be a dancer in a ballet company. Holidays take me back."

The woman smiled and was impressed. "I've come to see the clock that we talked about on the phone."

"Yes," I told her. Chesterfield and Moe had scurried away and had made me look foolish.

The woman probably imagined that I was talking to myself if she saw me through the window. "I have cats," I told her. "Their names are Chesterfield and Moe."

"How nice," the woman said. "I am in a hurry. Could I see the clock that you told me about?

"Yes," I said. "It's right here." I went behind my desk and lifted the ship onto the counter. "It's in good shape, works. Let's plug it in. Then you see it has its own navigation lights, red and green. The lights reflect off the stainless sails and you've a real unusual piece."

"How old do you think it is?" the woman asked.

"It's from the 1950s sometime, sometime around then. Not a very old piece but old enough to be considered an antique. I was dancing in the 1950s, was a star in those days."

"Really?" the woman said. "Yes really," I snapped at her. Then I regained my composure. "It would be just right to set on a television."

The woman opened her purse. "How much?" she asked.

I told her thirty-five dollars. She reached in her bag and pulled out her wallet. She didn't balk about the price. I should have asked for more. I noticed a huge diamond on her finger.

"Will you back it?" she said.

"Oh, you mean, will I swear that it keeps the time? Oh yes," I told her. She took the clock and was gone. I felt very sad, the ship was gone; gone were its clever red and green lights.

"Chesterfield and Moe, you can come out now. See boys, it pays to wait for callers. You think I'm an old woman that doesn't know her stuff anymore. But I proved to you that just isn't the case." I locked the shop's door. I went back to the player and put on music, Chopin, a piano concerto. The snow was piling up on the walk, and I was glad that tomorrow was Christmas. Nobody would slip and fall. Nobody would be shopping on Christmas.

I held Chesterfield and went back to my upholstered chair. Moe could just do without my attention tonight. "Chesterfield," I said. "It's sad to have things go. I'd like to have my things forever." I pulled the tabby to me, curled up, and fell asleep. The ship was in my dreams.

I lifted the end of my dress and twirled around Galveo's globe. Nanny looked at me, wondering about the cause of my joy. "I'm going back to Rawhoo," I told the she-goat. "I'm going to dance and have parties."

I stooped beside the globe and then gathered it in my arms. I let my hands run all over its colorful surface. I heard commotion on the deck above me. Footsteps moving down the stairs.

"Trinket," Nic called to me. "Trinket, unlock the door!" I hurried the globe to the back door and set it outside the supply area, in a dark space. I went to the other door to see Nic.

Nic burst through the entry and now stood in the supply area. "The captain is missing her prized globe." She grabbed the ladder, climbed up its steps, and shined her oil light on the shelves.

"I don't know about the captain's globe," I told her. "The captain never said anything to me about a globe."

"Galveo has sent me here. She's ordered a search of the entire supply area. She is with Sella at the moment. The captain is on her way, and we will find her lost globe." Nic came down the ladder and held her lantern high. She went back and forth, searching the lit space.

"Why Nic," I said. "There are splotches on your face, bright red pocks," I told the mechanic.

Nic stopped in her steps. Her hand went to her cheek. "Are you warm?" I asked. I put my palm on her forehead. "You're sick. You're sick, you're sick!" I said. "You ought not be out on the damp night without a cure. Let me give you a cure." I went up the ladder's rungs and brought down a small container. "Chew these," I said. "Chew these leaves twenty times."

The mechanic stroked her face, feeling for a rash. "The remedy must be taken at once," I said. Nic spun on her heels, holding the lantern high, looking at the shelves. "Please don't wait to take the cure," I said. Nic emptied the container into her hand and popped the bogus leaves into her mouth. "Now go rest," I told her. "The cure will not work without sleep."

"No globe," Nic muttered. I'll report to Galveo that her prized globe isn't in the supply area." She looked worried. "Twenty times?" she said. "Then do I swallow the leaves?"

"The cure will be stronger if you do," I said. Nic looked at me and felt safer with my words.

She smoothed her face, rubbing her cheek with her free hand. "The globe is not here," she said. She lowered her oil light and went quickly through the same door through which she had entered.

I took Nanny's muzzle into my hands. "We must go," I told her. "We must pack the landing boat and return to the island. We have the globe, Nanny. We'll find our way back. Oh, you're no help," I whined. "What use is a silly goat when they're going to be looking for us?" I ran to the back steps and up the stairs with the globe in my hands. I had to get the globe to the landing boat before I was found. The stars greeted me with their light and put down their spectacle in glints upon the ship's hardware. I saw Galveo and Sella on the bow. They were far ahead of me, but the ocean was still and the night was quiet.

The globe fit perfectly in the center of the landing boat's V. I placed it with care so as not to disturb the captain and the navigator. A captain's voice can be heard anywhere on a ship, and her distinct tone was soft but clearly spoke her love to the navigator. Yet I was in a hurry and had no time to listen to the captain's gentle words. Nanny would be waiting for me.

I slipped back down the stairs and was now in the supply area. I wanted to take my perfumes and my bottles. I stuffed them into a sack. My beads! How could I leave my necklaces and my bracelets. I needed food. I needed water. I had to pack fodder for the nanny. I could hear many footsteps now. I heard the helmswoman's voice. I heard her heavy steps.

I grabbed Nanny's leash. I heard the captain's voice. I heard Sella's. I heard the scribe's. I pulled the hesitant goat and made her climb the stairs that led to the landing boat. Sadness filled my heart. I was leaving the best of my things, so many glass beads, so many shiny bells and looking glasses. I thought my heart would break. Still I had to go back to the island.

When I was at the top of the stairs, I heard Galveo order that the door be opened. I pulled Nanny across the deck and with greater ease than what I expected she walked up the landing boat's plank. I threw the sacks with my few provisions over the sides. I hoisted the landing boat's pulley and lowered the small vessel into the night sea. The once calm ocean was now choppy and intent on tossing the craft. I let loose of Night Ship.

A fantastic space came between my small vessel and the Night Ship. The gap became larger and larger and was filled with moonlight. I held the nanny in my arms, feeling her rough coat. The ship's evening lanterns were becoming faint from distance, and the sea seemed to push me away, as if it knew the way back to Rawhoo and my island. Drums summoned me, and I was not afraid of the nothingness that surrounded me. Back, back, back. The strings of flowers. Blossoms. The clicking shells. I shut my eyes, was almost there.

Galveo

I delivered the Christmas prayer, a song that had been written by the scribe for this day alone. "Bring the joy of that first Christmas into our hearts; let our gladness now extend to the heavens and bring true fellowship on earth." My own personal prayer was along those lines: let gentle things be.

We are instructed that Christmas is a celebration of love. We bring out our gifts to rehearse the gift that God gave the world. I received a potted rose bush from Sella, and I looked forward to the blooms and the delicate petals. I gave the navigator a new silver compass and astrolabe.

Sadly our year had been marked by one misfortune; dear Trinket rowed out to sea, taking the mysterious globe. Despite our arduous efforts to find her, despite our back-tracking search, she was lost.

The crew tied streamers from the yards to celebrate the birth of Christ. Night Ship rolled forward in tropical waters; the sea was deep blue from its reflection of the sky, the clouds were angled and white like blown sails. It was Christmas, a festive day that we had waited for. It reminded us of our continent, our homes, where confections and cakes were being baked. Their dreamed aromas filled our nostrils, the sea and home joining in our minds.

Afterword

Since its original publication in 2003, *Night Ship: A Voyage of Discovery* has become a steady favorite with women's studies programs at universities across the country. Readers delight in the six women explorers who set out in search of new lands. Of course, they wonder if Galveo and Sella are still happily in love and about the fate of the Night Ship.

A few readers have suggested a sequel, thinking that there is more to tell about the sailors. I resist the notion. For me, Night Ship is a unique Christmas tale. It might be faithfully re-read every Christmas for what it says about love and the holiday. It tells stories about our earliest loves and the loves we search for later in our lives. *Night Ship: A Voyage of Discovery* was a joy to write. I hope new and old readers feel that emotion in the text and will continue to imagine the adventure.

Mattie McClane, 2017